This very spicy read gives a beautiful exposition of one woman's journey into an erotic world that she knew very little of… There are very hot scenes that demonstrate some of the techniques that can be applied but this is also a delicious love story and I look forward to reading more titles from this gifted author. ~ *Night Owl Romance*

Sierra Cartwright's In His Cuffs is a very sexy story. Maggie is a submissive who is experienced in BDSM play and knows what she wants. One of the things she wants is to enjoy her visits to the BDSM club and forget all about her business troubles, which includes a man who bought her mother's business and is now her boss… This is a good continuation of Ms Cartwright's Mastered series and I look forward to reading more. ~ *Ms Condit Reads Books*

I really enjoyed Sydney Wallace. She's intelligent, saucy and has just enough baggage to be multi-dimensional. Michael is intense, patient and solid…just what Sydney needs. The pace was brisk enough, and the sex was spicy and molten… Over the Line is a delicious erotic read for all fans of BDSM. ~ *Fallen Angel Reviews*

Totally Bound Publishing books by Sierra Cartwright:

Mastered
With This Collar
On His Terms
Over the Line
In His Cuffs

Signed, Sealed & Delivered
Bound and Determined
Her Two Doms

Anthologies
Naughty Nibbles: This Time
Naughty Nibbles: Fed Up
Bound Brits: S&M 101
Subspace: Three-way Tie
Night of the Senses: Voyeur
Bound to the Billionaire: Bared to Him

Seasonal Collections
Halloween Hearthrobs: Walk on the Wild Side
Homecoming: Unbound Surrender

Clasndestine Classics
Jane Eyre

Mastered

FOR THE SUB

SIERRA CARTWRIGHT

For the Sub
ISBN # 978-1-78184-657-5
©Copyright Sierra Cartwright 2013
Cover Art by Posh Gosh ©Copyright October 2013
Interior text design by Claire Siemaszkiewicz
Totally Bound Publishing

Published in 2013 by Totally Bound Publishing, Newland House, The Point, Weaver Road, Lincoln, LN6 3QN, United Kingdom.

Totally Bound Publishing is an imprint of Total-E-Ntwined Limited.

FOR THE SUB

Dedication

For ELF with thanks.
And for everyone who takes the time to connect with
me through social media. Your emails and messages
are a constant source of joy and inspiration. I
appreciate you!

Chapter One

"Another drink, Sir?"

Startled out of his reverie by the softness of a woman's voice, Niles looked over the rim of his empty glass. Brandy, one of the house's submissives, stood in front of him, her legs close together, her shoulders pulled back in a sexy way that thrust her chest forward.

Had he been so lost in thought that he hadn't heard her approach? Or were her movements so graceful and perfect that she'd managed to silently cross the Den's patio?

Given her seductively high stilettos, he doubted the latter.

Her long blonde hair flowed over her shoulders and down her back. Tonight she wore a short, slinky black dress that covered everything, but she seemed more intriguing because of it. The material clung to her, highlighting her ample breasts, trim waist and curvy bottom. This woman—sub—appealed to every one of his masculine sensibilities.

Her legs were bare, and her black heels emphasised the feminine shape of her ankles. For a moment, he fantasised about placing her on her back, removing her shoes then stroking his fingers against her instep before applying a cane to the soles of her feet.

He shook his head to banish the image.

It had been years since he'd played with a woman in anything other than a detached way. In fact, it hadn't happened since the tragic death of his beautiful, accomplished wife and sub, Eleanor.

But right now, he was thinking about touching Brandy in a way meant for their mutual satisfaction.

"Sir?" she asked, tipping her head. "Master Niles?"

The motion swept her hair to the side, snaring his interest. The locks were long enough, he mused, to be used as part of a hot bondage scene.

"Would you prefer to be alone, Sir?"

"Actually, no." The answer surprised him.

A month ago, he'd declined the invitation to tonight's party. Every fall, Master Damien hosted a get-together for Doms and Dommes who had been members of the Den for at least seven years. It was a small, select group, and they gathered to play poker, sip the finest single malt on the planet, enjoy conversation and, if they chose, scene with house subs. Not many people availed themselves of the playrooms, however, as most were in relationships, and this exclusive gathering focused on socialising, which was not his strong suit.

Damien had pestered Niles to the point of annoyance.

Despite his reluctance, and tired of his own company after spending a week at home by himself, Niles had acquiesced.

But after half an hour of mindless white lies, telling his friends and acquaintances that he was well, he'd made his escape to the solitude of the patio. He'd dragged a chair close to the crackling fire pit to enjoy the sunset. Today had been a mild day, and summer was breathing her last gasps before surrendering to the inevitable shorter, colder, bleaker days.

Brandy, a natural submissive, rather than one who'd been trained for it, cast her gaze down at the ground before looking up him. "I never said thank you for what happened at the last Ladies' Night."

"No thanks necessary," he assured her. "Any Dom would have done the same thing."

Many times, there was an assumption among new Doms that subs wearing the house's purple wristband welcomed any attention. A first-time visitor had made that error with Brandy.

Master Damien had not served alcoholic beverages at Ladies' Night, opting for froufrou, sugar-laced umbrella drinks that the ladies seemed to like. But that hadn't stopped the guest from drinking before he'd arrived.

Even when Brandy had used the Den's safe word, the asshole had continued on, forcing her to her knees and shoving his dick in his mouth. Niles had noticed her distress and stepped in.

Truthfully he'd enjoyed throwing the wannabe Dom out of the front door. The physical altercation had dissipated some of the angst churning in his gut, emotion he hadn't been able to get rid of otherwise. If Master Damien or anyone else had witnessed the uppercut Niles had delivered to the guy's jaw, no one had mentioned it.

Seeing his bruised knuckles the next day had been satisfying, but not as rewarding as watching the current, exquisite expression of gratitude on Brandy's face.

He rolled the empty glass between his palms, keeping his hands busy so he didn't yield to the temptation to reach out and touch her.

Niles realised he knew little about her. He'd seen her around the Den for years. She was always unfailingly obedient, but she didn't stand out. No wonder Damien continued to have her at his events.

"If you'd like to go to one of the private rooms, Sir, I'm available."

His cock hardened. He met her gaze. Her blue eyes were wide open and she gave him a quick smile that slammed his solar plexus. *Fuck.* Why had he never appreciated how attractive she was? Maybe because she wasn't the type he usually went for.

At six feet tall, his wife had looked him in the eye when she had donned the heels he liked. She'd been runway-model thin, with deep brown eyes and raven hair styled in a sleek, no-nonsense bob.

The two women couldn't be any more different.

Suddenly, though, the thought of bending Brandy over, making her scream his name as she came, stoked every one of his dominant urges. Still, he didn't want to scene just because she had a misplaced sense of gratitude. "You owe me nothing."

"I think you misunderstood. It was an invitation, Sir." She linked her hands at her back.

Interesting. Brandy was well trained, a perfect sub. And if he wasn't mistaken, she'd tucked her hands out of sight so he couldn't see the way she was fidgeting.

"I'm afraid I was being bold," she said, still looking at the ground.

So she was nervous, and he understood why. Though she was often summoned to the dungeon, he was certain she initiated few, if any, of the scenes. "I respect a woman who asks for what she wants."

As he stood, he put down his glass. Brandy didn't glance up. He placed his forefinger beneath her chin and tipped her head back.

She smelt of cinnamon with a tangy undercurrent of arousal. The spicy scent intrigued him. He'd expected something more floral, in keeping with her femininity. For the first time since Eleanor had passed, he wanted to scene for pleasure. "I accept," he said.

Brandy smiled.

The slow, sensuous curve of her lips made something deep inside start to melt. "After you," he said.

She scooped up his glass and started towards the main house. Her hips swayed from side to side, not in an exaggerated movement, but with natural feminine grace. He was looking forward to getting her naked.

Responding to a male instinct as old as time, he placed his fingers against the small of her back.

Gregorio, the Den's caretaker, opened the patio doors for them.

"We'll be availing ourselves of one of the playrooms," Niles said.

Gregorio drew his dark eyebrows together. Obviously, he hadn't been expecting that news.

"Let me know if you need anything," Gregorio said. "You as well," he said to Brandy as he accepted the glass from her.

"I'll take good care of her," Niles promised.

"See that you do," Gregorio said.

He appreciated the way Master Damien and Gregorio ensured everyone's safety, but this time it rankled. Niles would do nothing to harm Brandy.

With a nod towards the watchful Gregorio, Niles guided her through the kitchen then down the stairs that led to Damien's elaborate dungeon. "He's protective," Niles observed.

"I'm an employee and a friend," she said.

Niles owned a production company that often filmed at the Den, and he'd appeared in a number of their videos. He knew the rooms well, all the apparatus that was available and each of the implements he could apply to her body.

He stopped at the bar and snagged two bottles of water before asking Brandy if she had any preference on which room to enter.

"Sir?"

Clearly she expected him to make the decisions. Under normal circumstances, he would. But this evening was anything but ordinary. "This was your suggestion," he told her. "So I'm betting you have an idea or two about what you'd like to have happen."

"In that case, Sir, first door on the right."

He nodded, pleased with her answer. Because of its sparseness, this was one of his favourite playrooms. A hook hung from the ceiling, and a chair stood off to one side, tucked beneath a padded bench. The far wall was dominated by crops, whips, floggers and a tawse handcrafted by Master Marcus. As with all the rooms, there was a small sink and counter, and a cupboard stocked with necessities, including wipes, lube, condoms and towels.

She entered ahead of him. He paused to seal them in relative privacy. At the Den, all rooms had a window cut into the door. Every interaction was observed by Gregorio or Master Damien, meaning there was no such thing as complete seclusion, a policy Niles endorsed.

When he turned, he saw her kneeling in the middle of the room, head bowed, hands on her thighs. The subs — male and female — that he professionally dominated were actors and models. Each act was scripted and choreographed, and each response was exploited to ensure maximum effect. Screaming, whimpering and begging were all expected from the participants — after all, no one wanted to pay money for a download in which the spankee was silent.

He was reminded that Brandy, too, submitted for a living, but there were no cameras, directors or second takes now. This was between two willing participants for no reason other than pleasure. "Stand, please," he said. "Hands over your head."

Niles drew her dress up, exposing her beautiful body, inch by perfect inch.

She wore a scrap of material that served as panties, and she had on a black shelf bra that lifted her breasts. "I'm a fortunate man tonight, Brandy."

"Thank you, Sir."

He offered her the garment. "Fold it and put it on the counter then return to me."

Wordlessly, she did as instructed. She stood in front of him, her legs spread slightly and her hands looped behind her back. The rapid rise and fall of her chest indicated she was not as relaxed as she appeared.

It might have been ego, but he liked to think that this might mean something to her. If it didn't, he could live with that. Passing an hour or two together would make the evening more pleasant than he'd anticipated. "I'd like you to leave on the heels for now."

"Of course, Sir."

As he unbuttoned his cuffs and folded back his shirtsleeves, he asked her, "How expensive are your panties?"

"Very," she said.

"Sorry in advance."

"Occupational hazard, Sir."

He crossed to one of the drawers and took out a pair of safety scissors. Almost every week, he cut the material from an actress. This, however, was different. She wouldn't be turning in an expense report for replacement lingerie. Well, not to his company.

She stood still as he slid the blunted end between her skin and lace. "Ask me to do it."

Brandy met his gaze. "Do it," she said. "Cut the panties off me, Sir."

He did. The useless scrap pooled to the floor. "I like a shaved pussy," he told her.

"I'm pleased you approve, Sir."

She'd given him a stock answer. Any sub, any time would reply with a variation of those words. From what he'd observed, her training had been complete, exquisite even. But something in the pit of his stomach yearned for more—demanded more—from her. Honesty. He wanted honesty.

Maybe, he told himself, this was the real her. But part of him wondered if she was different away from the Den.

Stupidly, belatedly, he looked at her left hand. No ring adorned her finger, not that that meant anything. "Remove your bra and drop it."

Without hesitation, she did so.

The room was silent, save the sound of his heartbeat and her shallow breaths. "Look at me and tell me what you want, pretty sub."

Their gazes collided.

"To please you," she said.

"Then stop with the expected bullshit."

She gasped. "I'm not sure what you mean, Master Niles."

"I think you do."

Over the course of several seconds, she licked her upper lip.

"Stalling?" he asked.

"No, Sir. I'm trying to figure you out," she replied.

"That might be the most truthful thing you've said yet."

"You're a Dom, a very experienced one." She took her time, making every word count. "I'm a sub."

"Is that why you approached me? Do you want me to treat you as if you're interchangeable with any actress on the planet? I assure you, I don't see you that way."

To her credit, she took her time in answering. He liked that she was deliberate.

"No. It's not."

"I don't have a script, Brandy. And if I did, I wouldn't follow it. I would rather you be real with me, and natural. I need you to open up." With the power of his will, he held her gaze captive. "I need to know about your limits, but even more, I want to know the things that quicken your pulse and the sensations that make you writhe in ecstasy. I demand your participation, but not your blind obedience. Those are my terms."

"You'll think I'm selfish."

"I'm willing to take the risk."

"In that case, Sir, I love any kind of flogging, but especially one on my pussy, followed by a long, hard fuck."

His cock throbbed at the passion in her words. When he orchestrated a shoot, he never had sex with the actors. He'd bring them off manually or with a toy, but he kept his dick in his pants. Over the years, that had added to his mystique. He wasn't interested in his reputation. He had one purpose — grow the company's revenues.

"The truth is, if you get into what we're doing, I get off." She paused and sighed, as if either trying to figure it out for herself or find words to explain what she meant to him. "The energy builds on itself." Her blue eyes lightened, radiating her inner enthusiasm. "I can scene with almost anyone and enjoy it as long as they do, too. I love my work at the Den."

Niles had underestimated her earlier. He'd figured Damien continued to have her at his events because she pleased his guests and didn't stand out, but she was more complex than that. Early in his business career, Niles had learnt that any employee with a heartfelt desire to please should be rewarded and retained. Damien had apparently reached the same conclusion, after all, even during times of economic hardship, the Den's membership had continued to grow, despite some hefty membership fees. "I'd be delighted to redden your cunt," he told her.

"Thank you, Sir."

Even though the answer was rote, her tone conveyed gratitude. He left her long enough to grab a pair of cuffs and to lower the hook. Without being told, she extended her arms. As he fastened the soft fabric around her wrists, he asked, "Do you want to use anything other than the club's safe word?"

"Halt is fine, Sir."

"Any slow word?"

"I can't imagine one will be necessary, Sir."

Niles was adept at pushing subs to the utmost limits. After all, that created the most compelling of all videos. But he also knew how to read a sub's non-verbal clues. He knew, often before they did, when they'd had enough. "Do you have any conditions or limits I need to be aware of?"

"I have no medical concerns. As far as limits, nothing that will leave a permanent scar."

He nodded and affixed the cuffs to the metal hook. "If at any time you're too uncomfortable, let me know," he said.

"Of course, Sir."

"Do you need a spreader bar for your legs?"

"That won't be necessary, Master Niles."

He knew she'd do anything he commanded, but he wanted her to be able to let go and surrender to his lash. "Would it make the experience easier or more pleasant?"

"Yes, Sir."

Already he was learning to look at her eyes for an answer. The depths were expressive and revealed more than her words and tone together. He saw her gratitude and anticipation. She was looking forward to this. He wondered if she often had the chance to just let go and enjoy herself. Since this was her job, it was her obligation to ensure the Den's guests had their needs met. Tonight, he wanted more than that for her. He was glad she'd approached him, rather than wait for another Dom to claim her.

Niles fetched a metal bar. As he knelt, she widened her stance to allow him to attach the straps to her ankles.

This close to her, he inhaled the unmistakable, sharp scent of female arousal. Unable to resist, he spread her labia. "You're already damp, pretty sub."

"Yes, Sir," she whispered.

He slipped a finger inside her hot pussy. She locked her knees. "It's okay to respond. In fact, I'd like it."

He pressed his thumb to her clit then pulled back.

"Nice, Sir."

He alternated between applying intense pressure and a glancing touch, keeping her off guard. She swayed in time to his fingering and the way he teased her clit.

"I'm getting wetter, Sir."

He backed off a bit. "Are you close to coming?"

"Yes, Master Niles."

Nothing surprised him. He'd been with women who could orgasm from the lightest of touches. Others were capable of multiple orgasms. There were some who required so much stimulation that he was grateful for the assistance of an electric vibrator. Each sub was unique, and he enjoyed finding the right combination of touches that would make her respond. "Should I get you off?"

"It's your choice, Sir."

"Of course it is." He slid his finger deeper before pulling out. With a rhythmic, rocking motion, he increased the frequency of his thrusts.

She whimpered.

So damn hot. Her pussy tightened around his finger and she moved as much as the bar permitted, encouraging him to put more pressure on her clit. Wanting to please her, he followed her lead.

"I'd like to come, Sir."

"I'm sure you would," he said in soothing tones at odds with the way he stimulated her.

Her whimpers became groans.

"Sir, I'm going to come."

"Not yet, you're not."

"Master Niles, I'm begging you to either let me come, or stop now, Sir. At least" — she dragged in a couple of rapid breaths — "slow down."

Ignoring her, he continued the relentless torment.

"Damn, Sir..."

Her beautiful walls all but convulsed around his finger. How was it he'd never scened with her before?

"This is a taste of what's to come, sub," he warned. He moved his hand to sting her pussy with a quick, vicious slap.

She called out his name and jerked her hips as she came.

He reached to put one hand behind her and another on her abdomen, steadying her. She was so far gone, trembling and moaning, that he wasn't sure she'd be able to keep her balance otherwise. He hadn't pulled the hook taut, so it offered little support.

Niles smiled. "You're so perfect, Brandy." He looked up at her. A fine sheen of perspiration dotted her chest, and she took a deep breath.

When she appeared to have herself under control she said, "I came without permission, Sir."

Like she had earlier, she tilted her head to one side. Rather than drawing her eyebrows together when she was puzzled, she angled her head. How long would it be until he knew all her responses? "Now I have a reason to punish you when I see you again," he said.

"Punish?" she echoed. "You're a fiend, Sir."

"Let's add disrespect to the list, shall we?" he mused.

"But, Sir —"

"Along with arguing."

"I..." She closed her mouth.

"Good choice."

Her head was still tilted, and he doubted he'd ever seen anything more charming. And he wasn't finished with her yet. "Your pussy is bright red," he said.

"It feels as if it's on fire, Sir. And that was from a single smack."

She sounded as if she were looking forward to more.

"Did you like it?"

"Mmm."

"I've heard that sound when women eat chocolate cake."

"That, Sir, was better than cake. Even though I wasn't supposed to come—"

He grinned. "Oh, I meant for that to happen, I promise you."

She was silent a moment before adding, "Thank you, Sir."

He placed his hands so that both were on her rear then moved his face between her legs. "Fuck my face, pretty sub."

Brandy was too well trained to question him or hesitate.

Instead she moved her hips. "Dear God, Master Niles..."

He liked the high pitch to her voice, as if her vocal cords were rubbed raw by desire. After easing one thumb a bit deeper in her ass, he sucked her clit into his mouth then released her to cover her pussy with long sweeps of his tongue. He liked the musky taste of her and the urgency of her responses. If she wasn't restrained, he had no doubt she'd dig her hands in his hair and hold his head prisoner. As it was, she had to count on him to support her weight as she ground her cunt against his mouth.

Her heat covered his face.

"Do me," she demanded.

Fuck. This woman was hot.

It had been so long since he'd felt this alive, this engaged, that he'd go a long way to please her.

He used his tongue as she moved her hips. She bent her knees to change the angle as much as possible and give him greater access. He slid his tongue into her dampness and she screamed.

"I can't hold off, Sir!"

In response, he forced his thumb all the way inside her tightest hole. She continued to press her pelvis forward, and he dug the fingers of his left hand into the soft flesh of her buttocks.

Without another warning, her body went rigid before she moved again in short, desperate little motions as she fought for her orgasm.

With his mouth, his touch, he helped her along.

She raised herself onto her tiptoes, and the slight shift forced his tongue deeper.

One of her heels slammed onto the floor, a sound of satisfaction if he'd ever heard one.

"That was sensational," she whispered as he drew away. "Thank you, again."

An intense flare of lust gnawed at his insides. Making subs shatter was his passion. But it was nothing more than a job. He never engaged. Instead, he held himself and his emotions at a distance. He used a critical and artistic eye to make the scene sizzle. This time, though, his focus was solely on her. "I think that's enough of an appetiser."

"Oh, Sir…"

After washing up, he returned to her.

Damn. He liked the way she looked there, naked, blonde hair a cascading waterfall and curves designed to accommodate a man's body. She looked beautiful, but not in the classical way he had always preferred.

Niles skimmed a forefinger across her cheekbone. "Would you like to continue?"

Instead of the usual response where she would defer to his decision, she said, "Yes, please."

The certainty in her voice stoked his craving for her.

He crossed to the wall and raised the hook, stretching her body taut, keeping her in place and wide open for him. "Comfortable?" he asked as he crossed the room to check her bonds and positioning. He knew erotic pain could trump real cramps, at least in the short-term. It was his responsibility to ensure she was free to enjoy his torture.

He walked around her, looking at her from every angle. "You're a beautiful woman, Brandy."

Her nipples were erect, as if begging for his touch. There was nothing clinical about the way he took hold of each and squeezed the pink flesh between his thumbs and forefingers. This was about her pleasure rather than for maximum effect.

With a soft sigh, she closed her eyes.

"Look at me," he instructed.

She complied right away.

"Good," he told her. "As much as possible, I want you looking at me. Talk to me, communicate with me. Scream, even."

"I'm not much of a screamer, Sir."

"Yet," he countered.

"Challenge on, Sir."

"Bratty sub."

"You could have ordered me to be quiet."

"No chance in hell." He couldn't remember anything this pleasurable in...perhaps years. "Any preference in floggers?"

"Thuddy, not stingy."

"So I can beat you for a good, long time?"

"Yes, please, Sir."

"It will be my pleasure."

Her eyes were wide. He saw expectancy in the deep blue depths. He and Brandy were more alike than he might have thought. What they had done had merely whetted her appetite, as it had his.

Chapter Two

More.

Instead of being satiated, Brandy felt hungry, and she wanted more.

Master Niles had said he had no script, but her body had responded to him as if they'd done this a dozen times in the past. It wasn't just the way he touched her, it was the relentless tone in his voice and his see-all expression. He'd pulled her tight, leaving little room to move. Her body arched towards him, stretched like a bow, seeking his attention, ready for him.

Earlier this evening, she'd opened the door for his arrival at the Den.

She hadn't been prepared for her reaction to him. She'd inhaled his scent, that of power and prestige. He'd looked at her, and she'd thought his hazel eyes were haunted by loneliness.

She'd scolded herself for being fanciful. For the past two years, she'd forced herself to toughen up and be more practical even though it went against her heart's demands.

Tonight, she hadn't been able to shove aside the indelible image of the pain etched in his expression. It had tapped the nurturing instinct that life had taught her to quell, pitting her need for self-preservation against the urge to trail her fingertips across his brow.

As she'd performed her duties, greeting guests, fetching drinks and accepting jackets, she'd thought of Master Niles and recalled the way he'd so competently handled the situation on Ladies' Night. There'd been no drama as he'd stalked over, grabbed the man who was starting to get rough with her and escorted him outside. No one had seen what had happened next, but the overenthusiastic newbie Dom had not returned.

Master Damien, Gregorio or a House Monitor would have stepped in the moment they realised something was wrong. But Master Niles had arrived first.

She knew she owed him nothing, but thanking him had seemed polite and an excellent way to open a conversation.

Until tonight, she hadn't considered sceneing with him. Of course she would have been delighted to if he had ever requested her services, but to her knowledge, he hadn't participated in any scenes since his wife had died.

Brandy had known the beautiful and elegant Eleanor. In addition to being a dutiful wife and sub, she'd had a prestigious law career. The woman embodied everything that Brandy was not.

Still, she was glad she'd gathered the courage to approach him. Even at the Den, there was a hierarchy amongst Doms. Master Damien owned the estate and commanded respect as a result. Because of the way he behaved, she had no doubt he was accorded that same attention anywhere he went.

Next on the list were long-time Doms who had earned Master Damien's regard. He invited some of those to serve as House Monitors.

Tonight, as he did once a year, he hosted an invitation-only party for long-time members and friends.

Master Niles ran a production company. Of course she'd heard rumours that he was a skilled handler and kept things professional. He didn't fuck any of the actresses, even if they offered. Now that she'd been with him, she didn't blame them for trying. His motions, his lack of hesitation, no-nonsense tone and oozing confidence had already exceeded her expectations.

Feeling greedy, she licked her lower lip as he crossed to the wall and selected a flogger. The purple leather strands were wide, and she knew she'd feel its impact like a caress.

"Do you like to have your breasts whipped?" he asked when he turned towards her.

"Yes, Sir," she said.

Master Niles stood there with a flogger in hand. His white shirtsleeves were turned back and he wore tailored trousers and stylish wingtip shoes. With his dark brown hair clipped in precise lines and the stern expression on his face, he was over six feet of pure dominant deliciousness.

Although he'd recently given her two orgasms, her pussy throbbed with anticipation. Many times, Doms wanted her to play a role. She might be a maid who'd forgotten to polish a piece of silver, or a schoolgirl who hadn't done her homework. She had a locker at the Den, stuffed with different outfits and shoes.

She had a lot of duties—the uppermost was ensuring guests enjoyed themselves. Doms asked her to show their subs how to do certain tasks, and sometimes they just wanted to be served. She liked most of it. As with any job, there were days that sucked, times she felt tired and wanted to go home to the comforting craziness that greeted her.

But Master Niles was different. He hadn't been focused on himself—he'd concentrated his attentions on her, giving her what she wanted, perhaps because she'd been the one to suggest they scene. Over the years, she'd been with dozens of Doms, enough to know this man had no equal.

With a flick of his wrist, he shook out the flogger. Brandy held her breath.

He walked around her, re-checking the restraints, running his fingers across her shoulders to ensure nothing was hyperextended. She forced herself to breathe instead of demanding he get on with it.

Stunning her, he wrapped his arms around her body, imprisoning her, one strong arm across her chest, the palm of his other hand pressing against her lower belly. The whip hung from one of his fingertips, the strands lying against her thigh. With the way she was tied and now held, she couldn't move.

Her senses swam as he lowered a hand to cup her left breast. His touch was masterful, and she surrendered to it...to him.

He rolled her nipple between his thumb and forefinger, his touch exquisite and light. He came in closer, and she felt his erection against her. She smiled at the proof he was as turned on as she was.

As he increased the pressure, he moved his other hand lower to cup her mound.

"You're so wet, Brandy," he said.

She closed her eyes so she could let herself go. "Yes, Sir."

"Tell me what you want."

"Rub my clit, Sir. Let me come."

"I might prefer that you don't orgasm so I can keep you on edge."

"Of course, Sir." She took a breath, a trick she'd learnt years ago at a class for new subs. It gave her a moment to sort through her thoughts and allowed her to not react without thinking. "Whatever pleases you, Master Niles."

Against her ear, he laughed. "You're a terrible liar."

"Sir?" She opened her eyes and didn't blink.

"Your leg muscles tensed. If you were a poker player, we'd call that a *tell*. What just came out of your mouth is in conflict with what you want."

She froze. In less than half an hour together, this man had figured out her reactions, better than she knew them. Even she hadn't realised she'd tightened her muscles.

"Relax," he urged. "I'll let you know what I expect."

He moved two fingers between her labia, her dampness serving as the lubrication for him to glide across her most tender flesh.

Because his touch was so compelling, she had no choice but to do as he said. As much as possible in the strict bondage, she surrendered to him, leaning back. "This is so sexy, Sir," she whispered. "Thank you."

At first, he used the gentlest of motions. As she became moister, he began to rub her clit and press into her. She moaned, urging him on.

For a few moments, he indulged her, continuing to manipulate her nipple while stroking her pussy. She pressed her toes into the ground. And the moment she began to moan, he dropped his hands, and she heard him take a step back.

"Perfect," he said.

What? Her body vibrated with arousal. She sucked in a breath then forced it out from between her clenched teeth. She'd seen some of his videos. He was an expert in dragging multiple orgasms from his actresses. There was no faking the way he left them shattered, sweating and panting.

"Your body will be even more responsive to the flogger."

"That's not possible, Sir."

"It is," he assured her.

He came around to stand in front of her again, and he pressed his damp finger to her lips. Dutifully she opened her mouth.

"Stick out your tongue."

When she did, he held up his finger, and she licked her essence from him. Their gazes were locked on one another's.

His earlier expression had vanished, and now his hazel eyes were darkened by intensity. She sensed— knew—he was thinking of nothing but her.

He allowed her to suck for a few seconds before pulling back his finger.

Master Niles gathered her hair and arranged it so it hung down her back.

Brandy saw Gregorio at the window. "We have company, Sir."

Gregorio opened the door and stepped inside. "Everything all right here?"

Both men looked to her for the answer. She appreciated that Master Niles hadn't spoken on her behalf. It indicated a level of respect that not all Doms showed. "Everything is great," she said. "Thank you."

"Mind if I watch?"

"Yes," Master Niles responded. "I want Brandy all to myself. Out, unless the lady says otherwise."

"I don't," Brandy said, looking at her temporary Dom.

Gregorio grinned, and his silver earring reflected the light from overhead. "Was worth a try."

"Waste of breath," Master Niles corrected.

Once they were alone again, she wondered if they'd lost their momentum, but Master Niles continued as if they'd never been interrupted.

"Keep your head tipped back so I don't catch your face with the flogger."

Following that direction was easy when he laid the leather strands on her right shoulder. They felt sensuous against her flesh, yet she knew each throng was capable of a brutal bite. The contrast made her shudder.

He drew the flogger down her body, making her already-inflamed nerve endings tingle. He repeated the process from the left side, leaving behind a trail of desire. "Nice," she murmured.

After taking a step back, he tantalised her with slow, measured flicks. He caressed her belly, her breasts and her pelvis with the thick strands.

He was masterful, and she allowed her body to go as slack as possible.

"You seem to enjoy this," he said.

"Yes, Sir. Very much, Sir."

Almost without her noticing, he increased the intensity of his strokes. They became harder and faster as he made a figure-eight motion with the handle.

Brandy moaned. She had applied for a position at the Den because she loved to serve and genuinely enjoyed sensual stimulation. She wasn't a masochist, but the tactile feel of leather, rattan and even a wooden paddle against her skin turned her on.

As he'd instructed, she tipped her head back so her torso was exposed to him. She closed her eyes then bent her knees a bit, letting the hook above her take more of her weight.

Master Niles continued to flog her, catching her nipples with the blazing ends of the strands.

"Yes..."

"Are you still with me?"

"I'm liking this," she whispered. It would take a lot for her to reach subspace. Even though Master Damien and Gregorio saw to everyone's safety, she rarely trusted anyone enough to let go of her emotional defences to the point she could retreat inside her own mind and focus on absolute nothingness.

She had no idea how long he worked her, crisscrossing her body. Perspiration drenched her back. She had no doubt he landed every stroke precisely where he intended.

"Now your pussy," he said.

"Oh, *yes*, please."

He moved to the side for a different angle. Brandy tightened her muscles, but there was no need.

He wielded the flogger with precision, striking her pussy with tender leather kisses. He didn't need to tell her to relax. Instead, he coaxed her into it.

As he had earlier, he flogged with the gentlest of touches. Within minutes, though, she was whimpering from the heady combination of pleasure and pain.

She was aware of him saying something, but she didn't respond, content to enjoy the ever-increasing torment.

As soon as she arched towards him, he changed tempo.

He whipped her breasts, snapping at her nipples and viciously licking her cunt. Her pussy had moistened from the pain and she wanted more. "Sir, Sir…" she pleaded.

"Gorgeous girl."

He dropped the whip and cupped her mons with his right hand.

"Bring me off, I beg you, Sir."

"It's my pleasure," he said, pressing his thumb against her clit and fucking her with three fingers.

"Damn, damn, damn," she said. His thrusts were relentless, his touch commanding.

"Ride me," he said.

For as long as she could, she did as he instructed. But she was so on edge from the eroticism of the beating and the way he'd left her unfulfilled a while ago, she was already at the end of her ability to hold back.

He tightened his grip in her hair. The way he immobilised her shattered the last of her control. Screaming, she climaxed.

She sucked in several breaths as she recovered. Tenderly, he cradled her head. After a few seconds, she opened her eyes.

His face was only inches away from hers. Though he wasn't smiling, he nodded in apparent satisfaction.

"Fuck me?" she asked, the words almost a plea.

His eyes narrowed. "I want to see you bent over a chair with my cock filling your pussy."

She shivered, and it was from more than the chill as her overheated body cooled. His tone was harsh, rough, in tune with the way he'd used her body, but at odds with what she'd ever seen from him before.

That haunted look still lurked in his hazel eyes, making them appear a shade closer to green. His complexity took her by surprise.

He let go of her hair but left her attached to the hook. She craned her head so she could watch him untie his shoes and remove his socks. Most men she'd been with would hurry at this point, but he didn't.

He unbuttoned his shirt, and she fantasised about doing that for him. He shrugged out of the material and hung it on a peg in the wall before unbuckling his belt. She expected him to pull the leather from the loops, but he didn't. Instead, he removed his slacks and form-fitting boxers and hung them next to his shirt.

His erect cock was much bigger than average, and her mouth watered. Over the last two years, she'd agreed to have sex with various Doms, though it wasn't a required part of her job. Never had she looked forward to it like she was right now.

He was sexy, lean. His biceps were well-defined, proving he worked out.

After putting on a condom, he dragged a chair over.

"I'm leaving the spreader bar in place."

"Of course, Sir."

He lowered the hook, and she anticipated that he would release her right away, but he massaged her arms and shoulders, taking his time bringing back her circulation, even though she was anxious to get on with the fucking. "Thank you, Master Niles," she said, hoping it might hurry him along. It didn't. The man moved at his own pace, she was learning.

Finally he released her cuffs and soothed her wrists by making tiny circles on her skin with his thumbs. The contact didn't feel perfunctory, as if it were something he was expected to do. Tension and soreness drained away.

"How's that?"

"You can come to my house and give me a massage any night after work," she teased. Then she added, "Of course, I'd reciprocate."

"Spoken like a sub who suddenly realised what she said and is now hoping she doesn't get a spanking."

"Yeah. There is that, Sir."

He laughed. This was progressing unlike any other scene she'd ever had. Sure, she'd had laughs with Doms before, but often it was a nervous sound. And she'd never been with anyone as solicitous as he was.

"Over the chair, Brandy. I want your ass in the air. Put your hands in the middle of the seat area, and get on your toes."

Since she was still restricted by the spreader bar, he helped her into position.

Her hair flowed everywhere, almost acting as a blindfold. Staying where he'd instructed wouldn't be easy once he was inside her.

"Your pussy is bright red and swollen."

"It feels like it, Sir."

"It's perfect." He parted her buttocks to expose her pussy even more. "Are you still damp?"

"Yes, Sir. I'm ready for you. Crawling out of my skin, wanting you to hurry, if I'm honest."

He pressed his cockhead at her entrance.

She struggled against the impulse to surge backwards and take more of him. Most of the time, Brandy had infinite amounts of patience. But the confident way that he handled her, aroused her, made her eager for more.

"Arch your back more."

With grace—a result of ten years of ballet lessons—she wriggled around, rising on her toes to take even more of him.

"Nice," he said. "Now remain still."

"Yes, Sir."

He held apart her butt cheeks with his powerful hands.

"Fuck me, Sir," she pleaded.

"Do you try to hurry all your Doms along, Brandy?"

She felt a fevered blush stain her cheeks. "I'm sorry if it comes across that way, Sir. It's not that I'm trying to rush you. I just…" She trailed off as he stroked in even deeper.

"Just?" he prompted.

"I saw your cock and wanted it in me," she confessed.

"You know how to get your way." He thrust his dick inside her.

"So good, Sir. So, so good. *More.*"

"Bossy sub." He moved his hands so that he was braced against her hipbones.

It took all her skills to remain in place when she ached to stand and lean back into him. Instead, she splayed her fingers and concentrated on his rhythmic motions.

He rode her hard, like she wanted, filling her, stretching her with his thick cock. She whimpered and cried. Her breasts swayed. Hair tumbled everywhere in wild disarray.

Over and over, he surged into her, bringing her to the knife-edge of need. "Please, Sir," she begged.

"Come anytime."

He held her hips imprisoned and it only took a few more thrusts for her to feel as if she'd been turned inside out. She screamed as she forced her buttocks back, demanding all he had to give.

She wasn't sure what he did, but he managed to change the angle, sending a second orgasm careening through her.

Her legs trembled. She almost lost her balance. It wouldn't have mattered—he was there, supporting her, holding her with one hand on her shoulder, the other beneath her ribs.

"I've got you," he said.

In the safety of his arms, she let go.

He pistoned his cock into her, deep and demanding. She was overcome with the shock of her own surrender, and she came again.

His grip on her tightened, and his fingers dug into her shoulders. His movements were less controlled. Though she was lost, she revelled in the knowledge he was close to coming undone.

Inside her, he stilled. With a loud, masculine exhalation, he thrust forwards while still holding her tight. He ejaculated in a discernible, repeated pulse.

Even when it was over, and her breathing had returned to normal, he didn't move. He kept his possessive hold on her. With other Doms, the scenes often ended the moment he came. For whatever reason, Master Niles continued to hold her.

"I appreciate how responsive you are," he said.

"I appreciate how generous you are, Sir."

Inside her still-heated pussy, his cock began to soften.

Slowly he released her shoulder. Rather than move away, he brushed her hair to one side then trailed his fingertips down her spine.

Only when his dick slid out did he step back.

In the absence of any instruction, she stayed where she was. Not that she was capable of moving, at any rate.

"I'll be right with you," he promised.

His voice sounded gruffer than she'd ever heard it.

Brandy began to chill, from the fact she'd been tied, from the exertion, from the absence of his body's heat. She heard the sound of water running and splashing. He returned to her within seconds. He ran a warm, damp cloth across her back and pressed a second to her pussy, dabbing her swollen flesh.

"How are you doing?" he asked.

"That feels nice. Thank you, Sir." No wonder the man's production company did so well. If models and actresses were taken care of so well, no doubt they'd want to return.

He released the spreader bar and the metal clattered against the floor. She shouldn't have been surprised that he crouched behind her and rubbed her ankles then her legs. "You're spoiling me, Sir."

"As it should be."

He continued to work his way up her legs then massaged her buttocks, back and shoulders before placing an arm in front of her and helping her to stand upright. Then he turned her to face him. They were only inches apart. He'd disposed of the condom and his cock was still impressive. The scent of sex hung in the air, thick and musky. Every part of her responded to him. She reminded herself he was a Dom, this was nothing more than a scene, and it meant nothing to either of them.

Still, a sense of self-preservation made her take a step back.

She stayed there for a moment, feeling unsteady after he'd released her.

His eyebrows were drawn together in a fierce line. Earlier, she'd thought his eyes had looked haunted. Now she was certain of it. The tiny lines beside his eyes seemed deeper than they had earlier.

She wanted to reach for him. Instead, she gave a wan smile and pretended nonchalance as she moved towards her discarded clothing. "Thank you, Sir. That was hot."

Brandy expected that he'd put on his clothes and leave the room, like other Doms. Instead, he scooped up her bra and held it.

"Let me help you."

She froze in place, two feet from where he stood. "That's really not necessary, Sir." In fact, she would prefer to be alone to gather her thoughts and recover her equilibrium. He was the kind of man she could fall for, and being near him increased that risk. "I can clean up the room while you re-join the party."

"It wasn't a request."

"I..." With him, she was navigating uncharted ground. Realising capitulation might get her out of the room faster, she said, "Anything you say, Sir."

She put it on and fastened the clasp behind her. He adjusted the lacy cups so that they cradled her breasts. The man knew his way around a woman's lingerie.

Next he offered her the dress. Once she had it over her head, he helped smooth it into place.

He finger-combed her hair, not that anything short of a brush and curling iron could tame the wildness of her tresses.

"One day, I'd like to use your hair in a bondage scene."

She'd had it pulled, gripped, yanked, but never experienced that. And it also meant he'd like to play with her again. "I'd like that, Sir."

He knelt and helped her into the heels, and she placed a hand on his shoulder to balance herself. She liked his attentions, and she could easily grow accustomed to them. Master Niles behaved differently from any other Dom she'd scened with since hiring on at the Den. He left her off-kilter.

As he stood, he picked up her ruined underwear then discarded it in the trash can beneath the sink.

Pretending she was unaffected by what they'd shared, she tidied the room before sanitising the flogger. She dragged the chair back into place while surreptitiously glancing at him.

To her, there was something unbelievably erotic about watching a man dress, and the more powerful he was, the sexier it was. Even when he was naked, he'd lost nothing of his aura of command, but now that his shirt was tucked back in, his cuffs buttoned, his shoes tied, he looked as if he should run an empire.

"Shall we?" He led the way to the door then opened it for her.

She lowered her gaze as she neared him.

"Brandy?"

"Sir?" She stopped.

He pressed his thumb beneath her chin and tipped her head back. "Thank you."

Earlier, she'd noticed lines of tension on his forehead. They appeared somewhat less prominent now. Though she was unsettled by their encounter, it seemed as if it had been good for him. "Thank you, Sir," she responded. Instinctively, she curled her fingers around his wrist.

They looked at each other for a few moments, and he appeared as if he were about to speak. Then he shook his head. He settled for, "I look forward to seeing you again."

Realising how intimate her touch seemed, she dropped her hand to her side.

Her pussy still throbbed, and heat lingered in a few places on her stomach where his lash had fallen. He'd been masterful and deliberate, and she knew a number of members who would benefit if he taught classes at the Den. In the past, some Doms had taken her breath away with the harshness of their initial strokes. But Master Niles, with the way he'd first trailed the strands across her body, had gradually worked her into the beating. It had lasted longer and been harsher than most others she'd endured, and she hadn't been aware of anything except the pleasure.

Then he'd ended the scene with a few gentle touches before helping her dress. The subs who scened with him were fortunate, and spoilt for other Doms.

His eyes were lighter now than they had been earlier, the shadows banished. The sight gave her untold joy. Then, recognising that she was allowing herself to feel something emotional for him, she took a mental step back. "If you'll excuse me, Sir?"

"With great reluctance," he said.

After giving him a half smile, she brushed past him.

Instead of returning to the party, she took a few minutes to freshen up in the small area with the ladies' lockers. Most times, after a scene, she went right back to work. But Master Niles' tenderness along with the momentary vulnerability she'd glimpsed in his face had unravelled her, making her forget the lessons of the past two years. She couldn't allow anyone's problems to occupy a large part of her mind.

By the time she'd tamed her hair, applied a fresh coat of mascara and shimmied into a pair of panties, Master Niles had left the Den.

Brandy resumed her duties with less enthusiasm than usual. She helped Mistress Catrina into her luxurious coat, and arranged the Domme's long, beautiful hair so it looked gorgeous against the faux fur. Dressed all in black, the woman was stunning, and the way she carried herself, like a supermodel, only made her more beautiful.

"Thank you, little one," Mistress said. "Makes me want to have you lick my boots."

Brandy lowered her head. "If it's Milady's wish."

"If I wasn't ready to depart, I'd like to sample you." Mistress Catrina gave a soft sigh that was every bit as dramatic as she was.

The woman looked different without a young, half-naked man at the end of a leash, but that was part of the purpose of tonight's gathering, a time for Doms and Dommes to relax without any draws on their attention. It appeared most were grateful for the opportunity, but even more eager to return to their submissives.

That made her wonder if Master Niles had anyone at home, perhaps waiting on bended knee for his arrival. To her knowledge, he was single and alone, but she knew little, if anything, about him. Suddenly she was hungry for more information.

An hour later, when Master Marcus was leaving, she held his leather bomber jacket while he shrugged into it.

"Shall I have your vehicle brought around, Sir?"

He shook his head. "I'm too impatient to wait."

She smiled at his abrupt tone, as if being away from home and Julia even this long had been torture. She opened the front door, and a blast of cold evening air smacked her.

"Autumn in the Rockies," he said, turning up his collar. "We're in for an early snow."

Once the sun had set, the temperature had plummeted. She slammed the door closed, and was grateful for the whisper of warm air from the heating vent.

Gregorio wandered into the foyer. "You're quiet tonight. Did everything go okay with Master Niles?"

"Fine," she said. "The man knows what he's doing."

"Don't get your heart broken," Gregorio warned.

She scowled. "What the hell makes you say that?"

"Nothing more than a lucky guess. I was feeling you out. Your response was a bit touchy."

"And you're more than a bit nosy," she countered.

"You can't fix everyone."

"Who said I want to fix him?"

"Don't you?" Gregorio challenged.

In his inimitable style, he folded his arms across his chest and spread his legs, standing there like an unmovable object. She knew better than to try to push past him. Tonight he wore a black T-shirt and black jeans with black motorcycle boots accented with sturdy metal buckles at the ankle. Though he could be a switch, right now, he looked fierce, protective of her.

"I'm sure that's the only time we'll ever scene."

"Why did you invite him?"

She bristled, feeling defensive. "Who said I initiated it?"

"Master Niles wouldn't have."

"You sound certain of that."

"I am."

Brandy sighed. "I'm not sure," she admitted. "Something in his eyes..."

Gregorio said nothing.

"I'm allowed to initiate a scene with the guests," she said.

"You are." He lapsed into silence again.

"Fine. I'll be careful."

"I love you like a sister."

She gave him a wan smile. "You're as big of a pain in the ass as a big brother would be." And he knew her as well as a family member might. She had dozens of friends, no close relatives and a fractured spirit. Gregorio had spent many long nights at the Den talking with her after all the members had left.

One evening, he'd sat on the couch with her while she'd spilt the secrets of her past with Darren and cried herself to sleep. She'd awakened before dawn. She had been snuggled against Gregorio's chest, and his arm was around her shoulder.

More than anyone, he had the right to question her motives with regards to Master Niles. Gregorio knew her past as well as she did, maybe even understood it better than she did. If and when her soul shattered again, he'd be there to pick up the shards.

"Promise me you'll be careful."

"It meant nothing to him," she said.

"You're right," he said, but his words lacked conviction. "Don't forget it." With that warning, he told the valet to fetch her car.

"I am on duty until midnight," she protested.

"You're going home."

"Working might be good for me."

"And being with your zoo is better."

"I prefer the term menagerie."

"Zoo."

She gave him a quick hug. He pulled out her coat from the back of the closet. After she'd put it on and fastened all the buttons, he walked her to her vehicle.

"You have my phone number," he reminded her.

"I won't need it." She fastened the safety belt across her lap. "You would annoy the hell out of me if I didn't love you so much."

"You annoy me because I love you so much." He closed the door and gave her a sharp salute.

Brandy struggled to stay focused during the drive home. When she arrived home to the insane welcome of barking and meowing, she realised why she'd been so defensive with Gregorio. He was right. She hadn't done a good job of being professional with Master Niles. She'd wanted to scene with him, be with him. But she'd wanted him to see her as a woman, not as a professional hired to do the job. Tonight she'd broken one of her cardinal rules. She'd allowed their time together to mean something to her.

Brandy turned on the radio and cranked up the volume, hoping to drown out her thoughts. She told herself that, by morning, she'd forget about him.

But for now, she allowed herself to remember the way he'd looked at her when he'd turned her to face him after fucking her so hard she'd all but forgotten her own name.

Chapter Three

"You should squeeze it gently to make sure it's firm, but not so firm that it has no give."

Niles looked up from the display of tomatoes and turned to face the woman standing next to him. "Brandy?"

"Vine-ripened are best," she added. "They're much better if they're not picked when they're green."

Here, in a small market in Granby, he barely recognised her. He hadn't expected to run into someone he knew, and this woman bore little resemblance to the woman he'd scened with a few weeks before.

She wore no makeup. Her gorgeous blonde hair was pulled back into a ponytail. She had on a black sweater and matching skirt, with black tights and comfortable-looking suede boots with some sort of fur cuff. A stunning magenta scarf completed her outfit. She took his breath away.

The scent of her, fresh, like a crisp autumn morning, walloped him. Images of her naked body tied up and waiting for him flashed through his mind, leaving him aroused and not at all convinced he wouldn't take her up against a wall.

"And make sure there are no external blemishes."

"Ah," he said. "Thanks." He put down the tomato he'd been holding and schooled his runaway thoughts. That night at the Den after he'd taken her to the dungeon, Damien and Gregorio had pulled him aside and explained that Brandy was an excellent sub and even better employee. More than that, Gregorio thought of her as a younger sister. Niles had assured both men that he had no intentions towards any woman, including her. But the way he was feeling this moment, with her standing a scant few inches from him, he sure as hell had ideas, and they weren't honourable. Reining himself in, he reached for some small talk. That's what polite people did when they were trying to pretend they were better than Neanderthals. "Is it that obvious I don't know what I'm doing?" And he might starve if he didn't eat out or have a housekeeper who shopped for him once a week.

"I'm sure it would have been fine."

"Really?"

"No. That was a lie." She shook her head. "It would have been tasteless, dull. Boring. And you don't like those things."

"You're right." Which explained a lot about his attraction to her.

"I didn't know you lived up here," she said.

"I don't. I'm staying at a friend's cabin. Most of the time he rents it out, but it's between seasons right now, no real hunting or skiing, and the summer vacation season is over."

"It's a great time for seeing the aspens," she said.

"And listening to the elk bugle. Do you live up here?" he asked.

"I do. I've been up here about two years. I left Denver after The Great Disaster."

"Taking it that's not a movie?"

She grinned. "It was a fresh start, and I've been lucky to find work doing some marketing for one of the smaller ski resorts and a couple of the towns around here, web design, social networking, that sort of thing."

Odd that he'd never considered that she had a job outside of being a submissive at the Den. Then again, over the last few years, he'd thought of precious little beyond what he'd lost. He wondered what she'd almost revealed before catching herself. For the first time in a long time, he was intrigued.

"Are you any good at barbecuing?" she asked.

"You're asking a man who can't select a tomato?"

"The two can't be compared. Men will cook if flames and risk are involved. It's genetic. A badge of honour, even."

He laughed. "That sounds sexist."

"Is it true?"

"I've lit a grill a time or two," he conceded. No way could he be considered a gourmet, though.

"With matches or a flamethrower?"

"Both. Why do you ask?"

She brushed her hair back from her face. "I'm having a small get-together this afternoon at my place. Nothing fancy. Just a few friends. But the neighbour who cooks the hamburgers had to go out of town. I need a replacement."

"You're asking me to be your chef?"

"Well, I wouldn't go that far. Cook is fine."

He socialised only with a select group of people he knew well and who didn't pry into his personal life or try to set him up with their available female friends. His friends understood his need to be alone, and they honoured it. This woman, though, had intruded on his privacy at the Den and now she was trying to drag him to a gathering where he knew no one. She was treading where no one else dared go.

"I bet you're wondering what's in it for you," she said.

He was actually trying to think of an excuse that wouldn't crush her and make him feel like a louse.

"Dinner," she said. "Everyone brings a dish, and you know how that is. No one brings things they're bad at. So there will be lots of salads, several kinds of dessert, including cheesecake, and all the beer you can drink." She cocked her head to one side and smiled at him. "And you'll have my undying gratitude."

The last part interested him.

"I'm desperate," she confessed, going on as if she'd sensed an opening. "Since I'm the hostess, I have a million things to do, and I know I'll forget about the burgers and burn them, or get impatient and take them off too soon." She looked at him with wide eyes, as if it didn't occur to her he'd refuse.

In her world, no doubt people did help one another. Niles had never been the neighbourly type. "Brandy, I don't—"

"They're a good group of people."

"I'm sure they are."

"I'll owe you a favour. Please say yes."

Good God. There was no way to refuse this woman anything. At the Den, he'd thought of her as a beautiful, compliant submissive. In this moment, he knew he'd underestimated her. She had the relentless determination of a bulldozer. But she'd approached him with such guileless trust that he wanted to help. "I can spare a couple of hours this afternoon."

"Yes. Yes, yes, yes, yes, yes." She did a little two step, and an older couple smiled at her enthusiasm. "Thank you, thank you. I'll even pick out your tomatoes. In fact, all of your produce. How's that for gratitude?"

Ten minutes later, his basket was full, he'd been educated about the reasons to select heirloom vegetables, learnt how apples were graded and she'd given him directions to her home.

"See you around three."

He realised she wasn't asking, she was telling.

Without waiting for an answer, she raised on her tiptoes and leaned towards him to press a kiss to his cheek. "Thank you, Sir."

She gripped the bar of her basket and strolled off with a little wave, making him wonder what in the hell had just happened.

He'd come into town for a few staples and a bottle of scotch, just a couple of things to get him through the weekend, and now a scrap of a woman who was supposed to be a submissive had commandeered his afternoon.

And damn if her small expression of thanks hadn't made him want to wrap up the moon and give it to her.

He didn't have to wonder how long it had been since he'd shared a small, intimate moment like that with a woman. To the minute, he knew. Until now, though, he'd thought he'd buried the ache under layers of regret. But Brandy, with her genuine delight and unrestrained appreciation, awakened a part of him that he'd thought was gone forever.

Sierra Cartwright

With a sigh, he headed for the junk food aisle and justified his action by telling himself potato chips were made from vegetables.

Niles hoped to run into her in the checkout lanes. If he did, he'd load her groceries into her vehicle. He didn't see her again, and he wondered why it bothered him.

After he arrived back at the cabin, he started to put away his food. He held the tomatoes and considered them. Refrigerator or countertop? Did it matter, really? Maybe it did. No doubt Brandy could write a dissertation on it.

Deciding to put them in the refrigerator so they'd last longer, he changed into a long-sleeved flannel shirt before heading outside to chop some wood to stockpile for the winter. Nights were already damn cool up here, and snow wouldn't be far behind. Doing physical labour was part of the reason he was allowed to use the cabin at no charge.

He skipped the chainsaw in favour of a good old-fashioned axe. He hefted the substantial weight and brought it down in smooth, powerful moves.

There were dozens of logs to cut, and he knew it would take his friend several weeks to get through them. That suited him fine. He needed the physical movement to banish the sudden and stark image of Brandy kneeling naked in front of him, her legs spread as she waited for his attentions.

An hour later, muscles straining, sweat beaded on his brow, he sank the axe head into a log and stood upright, stretching his sore muscles. He opened the top couple of buttons on his shirt before striding back inside.

Even though he'd drained his energy, the physical exertion hadn't helped. He saw the rug and pictured her there.

He showered, masturbating as he stood beneath the warm water. Ejaculating didn't vanquish the sexual energy he felt when he thought of her. In fact, it seemed to make it worse.

Niles set the spray to a hot, punishing pulse that hammered his shoulders. As he stood there, the truth hit him. Brandy's curvy body and long, blonde hair appealed to him. When he factored in her direct communication and the way she'd kissed his cheek, as if it was a natural impulse, he was done for.

No way should he attend the function at her house.

He didn't want to meet her friends, answer curious questions or learn anything more about her. If he went to the party, people would assume they had a relationship. He needed to keep her outside his inner circle. They could hook up at the Den, then he could walk away at the end of the evening having dominated a willing, sexy submissive. Wasn't that every man's fantasy? A hot woman in the bed and no awkward moments afterwards?

Niles turned off the faucet.

Truth was, he wanted to know her better. He wanted a glimpse of her in her natural element, surrounded by fun and laughter. All the things he'd told himself he shouldn't want.

Rather than drying off, he wrapped a towel around his waist and strode to his closet to grab a tight-fitting pair of boxers from a chest of drawers.

He selected a pair of newish jeans and a long-sleeved, metal-grey T-shirt. Since he was going to be relegated to the outside, he reached for a pair of hiking boots. Definitely not his usual attire for a date.

Not that this was a date. He was in charge of the grill. Nothing more.

An hour later, in his sports utility vehicle, he repeated that affirmation aloud. Then he wondered if he'd always been so good at lying to himself.

Only one car was parked in her driveway. He'd timed it so he'd arrive early, and he was glad he had.

When he stepped out of the vehicle, he was greeted by a cacophony of barks, one ferocious and the other one a higher pitch, but lower volume.

Should be an interesting night. After grabbing the bottle of wine he'd brought as a gift, he headed for the house. It was a cottage-type with two doors, one at the front and another on the side. A silver metal tub filled with ice and beverages stood beneath the carport, so he surmised that was the way to party headquarters. A moment later, she flung open the door and greeted him with a broad smile.

"Master Niles," she said. "Welcome to my humble abode." She looked at the two dogs that were doing a small dance behind her and commanded, "Stay back."

The animals obeyed, but continued to vocalise their excitement and wag their tails.

He'd wondered how she would greet him, especially as she would be having other people over. But like the perfect submissive, she still observed his minimum protocols.

Niles extended the bottle of wine. Their fingers brushed as she accepted.

"Thank you. You didn't need to bring anything. You're the chef, not a guest," she teased.

"I was hoping this would work as a bribe," he said. "Maybe someone else can cook while I eat those desserts you mentioned."

"No chance, Master Niles. This afternoon, you're all mine to command."

She kept a straight face for all of three seconds before grinning. They both knew he was a Dom and wouldn't relinquish that role. Still, her easy banter made it easy to relax, and he was glad he'd come.

"Shall I uncork it for you, Sir?"

"I'll do the honours, if you don't mind."

"Of course, Sir. Thank you."

She stepped aside so he could enter the kitchen. Since the tiling on the floor was worn, he presumed her friends and family all used this same door, and that added to the welcoming feel.

Now that he was inside with the door closed, the dogs bounded over. One was a massive brindle the size of a pony and had a pink bandana around her neck. The other was an overweight, black, snarling Dachshund.

"I would have warned you about my menagerie," she said, "but I didn't want to scare you off." She waved her hand, about waist level and both canines quieted. "That's MW," she said, pointing at the smaller dog.

"MW?"

"Meanie Wienie."

He laughed.

"I don't want to give him a complex, so I just call him MW." Brandy placed the bottle of wine on the counter and retrieved a waiter's corkscrew from a drawer that contained several hundred gadgets he'd never seen before.

"Since it's not summer, it's not a big concern, but he has an, uhm..."

Niles waited.

"Foot fetish, of sorts. He bites big toes. Not ankles. Not feet. Just toes, big ones."

"Rescue dog?" he asked.

"How did you guess?" she replied with a wry twist to her mouth as she placed the corkscrew next to the bottle. "They're one of my weaknesses."

That she collected unwanted animals didn't surprise him. He suspected her heart had melted in a similar fashion at the Den when she'd caught sight of him sitting outside by himself. "Do you do it with humans, too?"

"Not anymore."

"Meaning you used to."

"Not much to tell," she said. "But you're right. I've spent a lot of time trying to break myself of that habit. Animals are far easier to deal with than people. They're more honest. Anyway, the Great Dane is named Dana." She shrugged.

"Original."

"A little girl chose it."

"I didn't know there were brindled Great Danes."

"I didn't either until the rescue service brought her to me."

"They're very nice dogs," he said.

Both animals, as if on cue, sat and offered their paws to be shaken.

"I try to teach them some manners. Success is measured in varying degrees."

Niles shook Dana's paw first, then he crouched to accept MW's. The animal promptly dropped to the floor, rolled to his back and offered his belly to be rubbed. "He likes attention."

"He'd get more of it if he didn't bite toes."

"He seems fine to me." After playing with the dogs, he stood to rinse his hands. Bowls and cutlery had to be moved aside, and she made no apology for her mess. The kitchen cabinets were painted white and complemented by dark blue laminate counters. Knick-knacks adorned the shelf beneath the window. An old-fashioned stove, oversized refrigerator and a battered dishwasher made the place feel homey, lived in. It was quite a contrast to his enormous space that was filled with stark granite, steel, strategic decorator lighting and brushed satin nickel fixtures. He might have felt as if he were out of his element, but that was impossible with how easy she behaved.

She moved in next to him and offered him a towel to dry his hands.

With the newcomer sniffed and welcomed, the dogs wandered over to their beds and curled up.

"Now that they're settled, may I offer you a beer? A bottled water? A glass of the wine you brought?"

"Wine."

"For me, too, if you're okay with sharing?"

"I was hoping you'd join me." He put down the hand towel then uncorked the bottle.

She removed two wine glasses from a cupboard, and he accepted them from her.

"We'll let it breathe for a minute," he said. "And in the meantime, you can greet me properly."

Brandy sucked in a breath and looked up at him. "Honestly, Sir, I've wanted to kiss you since you walked through the door."

There was that raw honesty he appreciated so much. He was glad he'd come.

She sank to her knees in the middle of the kitchen.

Everything about this woman turned him on. She still wore the short skirt that showed the curve of her hips. While he liked the sight of a woman's bare legs, he had to admit the boots and tights were doing it for him. Getting her naked later would be even more rewarding. The sweater clung to her breasts and hid her gorgeous nipples. Despite the fact they weren't at the Den and this could be considered outside the bounds of normal behaviour—after all, they hadn't discussed how she would treat him—she hadn't hesitated before kneeling. "How long do we have until the rest of your company arrives?"

"At least half an hour, Sir."

He offered his hand and pulled her up before removing the band that secured her hair. The long waterfall of blonde fell past her shoulders in a gentle wave. "I meant it when I said I want to restrain you that way sometime."

"Since you mentioned it, Sir, I've fantasised about it."

"Then I'll have to make sure it becomes a reality."

"Thank you."

He captured the hem of her sweater and pulled it up over her head.

"Pale blue?" he asked, seeing her bra.

"I figured you would expect me to go for black or red. So I wanted to surprise you."

"You succeeded." Again and again. This sub—woman—intrigued him. Her spontaneity kept him guessing.

He'd wanted to be sure—that night at the Den—that she hadn't offered to scene because of a misplaced sense of obligation.

At the grocery store, she could have pretended not to notice him. Instead, she'd approached him and made up an excuse that compelled him to attend her party. Over the last few years, he'd had models and actresses drop suggestive hints about hooking up, but the fact Brandy had only asked him to attend as a friend had snagged his attention and reeled him in.

"Since you didn't give me any instructions, I went with lady's choice."

"Well done," he assured her. "The colour works." The gentle pastel complemented her porcelain skin. He'd never have known he liked anything other than bold or bright.

"You might want to put the sweater on the counter or the table, Sir," she suggested. "Otherwise, MW will think it's his new blanket."

"I've never had to consider pets when I took off a woman's clothes."

"Is that a problem?" She drew her eyebrows together.

"Relax, gorgeous sub." He ran his thumb across her forehead. "I have no issue with your four-legged friends."

"Good. Because you haven't met them all yet."

"There's more?"

"More of everything for you, Sir."

"Then let's get on with it." He reached around and unfastened the clasp of her bra.

She shrugged from the straps, and her luscious breasts spilled into his palms. His cock hardened right away. He should have masturbated a second time before leaving his cabin.

"Thank you," she murmured as he lightly squeezed.

"They need to be marked."

"God, yes, they do, Sir."

It seemed her passionate intensity matched his. Even though she was distracted, she somehow managed to deposit the brassiere right on top of her sweater.

He fondled her nipples until they beaded then he pinched them hard.

"You're making me wet, Sir."

"Good." He hitched up her skirt and placed one of his legs between hers. He dragged her closer and held her tight. "Hump my thigh like the horny, greedy woman you are."

She looked up at him. Her eyes darkened to the colour of a still, deep mountain lake. Without a word, she leaned into him, wrapping her arms around his neck before manoeuvring her pelvis so that her clit would be stimulated, even through their layers of clothing.

He supported her weight as she began a slow, rhythmic rocking motion. Niles cradled the back of her head then dug his fingers into her hair. He'd effectively imprisoned her, and he never wanted to let go.

"Oh, oh, Sir."

"I want your orgasm, Brandy. Give it to me."

Her breath felt warm on his chest. She moved faster and faster. Having her in his arms seemed inevitable. Despite the difference in their sizes, the fit was perfect. "That's it," he told her. Then he moved one hand lower and brutally slapped her ass.

She screamed. It wasn't from the pain, he knew, but from the force of her climax. Her body went limp, and he brought her against his chest while she caught her breath.

"That... Thank you, Sir." She looked up at him. "I had no idea you'd let me do that."

"Me either."

"Honestly?"

"I've spent plenty of time thinking about doing you." Even though he shouldn't have. If he hadn't been warned off by Damien, Niles would have gone back to the Den to seek her out.

Brandy swallowed.

By slow measures, he released the tight grip he had on her hair. "But when you opened that door, I couldn't be a gentleman and wait until later. And I couldn't torture you, even though I'm being tormented." Her body was designed for explosive sex. "I'd prefer to have an entire afternoon to play with you, but having you ride my leg will have to do."

"Thank you for the orgasm, Sir. I might have snuck off to the restroom, otherwise." She lifted herself onto her tiptoes, leaning against him more. With her lips parted, she reached her hand around his neck and drew his head down a bit.

He never allowed subs this much liberty, yet he was helpless to resist her.

Brandy pressed her lips to his. Then, with boldness he should have expected, worked her tongue into his mouth, seeking and searching, learning.

He loved the enchanting way she led, the taste of her, that of sensuality and longing. Before long, his natural personality asserted itself and he took over. He pulled her head back and forced her mouth open wider.

In surrender she moaned.

He plundered, loving having her heated body against his. He all but fucked her mouth with his tongue in an unspoken promise of what would happen later.

"Damn, Sir," she said when he set her away from him.

"Beware," he warned her.

"Sir?"

"You may want to keep a safe distance from me during your party."

"Can't keep your hands to yourself, Sir? I would have thought you had more self-control."

"If you'd like to continue with the sass, you'll find yourself over my lap with your derrière upturned, regardless of whether we're alone or with company."

"Bring it on, Sir. I'm not afraid of your little spankings."

This woman was so unlike other women— submissive or not—that he'd been with. She knew how to behave and responded with perfection to every command. But she lacked the artifice that he'd become accustomed to. A lot of women he'd been with played subtle games with flirtation, pulling back when he showed an interest. Brandy let him knew what she wanted and she took the initiative to get it.

Never one to make idle threats, or indulge a disrespectful wench, he reached for a kitchen chair. Her eyes widened.

He didn't say a word as he sat and dragged her across his knee.

She laughed in apparent delight. The dogs jumped up and barked as if they wanted to join the fun. She commanded them into silence, and they both lay back down.

Niles trapped her legs between his and pulled her skirt up to her waist. Mindless of whether he caused a run in her tights or not, he pulled those down to mid-thigh level. He yanked her thong tight between her buttocks. *Christ.* Her ass was even more round and delectable than he remembered. In this position, with her light blue underwear separating her ass cheeks and dark tights framing her legs, her body seemed even more inviting.

He almost succumbed to the temptation of rubbing her skin and bringing her off again. Forcing himself to focus on his intention, he brought his hand down hard on her creamy flesh, creating an instant, harsh slash of red. "Still laughing?"

"No, Sir." Her voice had changed. Mirth had vanished, as if she had sudden clarity of the grievousness of her behaviour.

Niles delivered half a dozen blistering strokes, continuing until she gasped. He knew she wouldn't cry or beg him to stop, and he heard her drag in some big gulps of air to help her settle into her spanking. Her tits bounced free, keeping him aroused. Damn, what she did to him…

Before she could get comfortable, he stopped then jostled her from his legs while grabbing her around the waist to help her to her feet. "Stand there," he instructed.

As he expected, she followed orders, contrite, eyes downcast, arms behind her back. The position pushed out her breasts, as if in offering. She made no attempt to rub her buttocks or right her clothing even though the tights had to be constricting her circulation.

For a full minute, he sat and observed her. How the hell had she started to matter to him so quickly? He'd had no intention of doing anything other than hanging out this evening as an invited guest.

But sparks were inevitable. She was like flame to his kindling. He'd had no idea how much he'd missed having a subbie around, the rightness, the interaction. They each needed what the offer offered. "Well?" he asked when he'd given her time to think.

"Thank you for the spanking. That should teach me to hold my tongue and not laugh when you initiate a punishment, shouldn't it, Sir?"

"Will it?" Niles stood and caught her chin. Without him having to instruct her, she met his gaze.

"Yes. I'd much rather have an erotic spanking," she admitted.

"I'm happy to indulge your taste for that."

"I misjudged the situation, Sir. On second thought, I realise that what I said could be considered rude, and that was never my intent. I apologise, Master Niles."

"Apology accepted. You may straighten your clothes." He watched as she wriggled and tugged on her tights then smoothed the back of her skirt into place.

He handed the sweater to her. "Do you have any objection to going braless?"

"My breasts are a bit on the large size, Sir, so I almost always have one on unless I'm at the Den. But if it's your pleasure, Sir, I'm happy to do as you wish."

"Then skip it. I want to see your nipples all night and imagine them in my mouth, in my clamps."

"Yes, Sir." She pulled the sweater over her head.

He untucked her hair from her collar. "How does your ass feel?"

"Sore. You've made your point. I will be more respectful."

"Are you ready for that glass of wine?" He splashed a small amount into one glass. After swirling the rich, red liquid around the bottom of the glass, inhaling the scent then sipping to confirm its taste on his palate, he poured them each a glass.

"It's more full-bodied than I anticipated," she said, making a funny little sound with her mouth.

"I like more than my wine that way."

For a moment, they were both silent. "Lucky for me. Shall I give a quick tour of the place? There's not much to see."

Before leading the way to the large living room, she snatched up the discarded bra. "I think this was a combination dining room and living room, but a wall was knocked down between them. Since I have an eat-in kitchen, I prefer to keep this as a great room, of sorts."

A large television was mounted on a wall, and she'd turned on the gas fireplace. In addition to the overstuffed couch, she'd set up a number of chairs and trays.

"What's in the aquarium?"

"Lizards. Zig and Zag. They're leopard geckos."

"Let me guess, someone else named them."

"Umm, no. That bit of creative genius was mine," she said, and blushed in a way he found endearing.

"I'm sure it suits them."

"Sir is being kind."

"Yeah," he agreed. "I am. Trying to be a good guest."

Brandy laughed before leading the way to her office. She propped a shoulder against the doorjamb and took a sip of her wine. This room surprised him. Her work space was uncluttered. A notebook computer sat on a glass desk. A couple of manila file folders were scattered near it, but other than a cup containing pens and pencils, nothing else adorned the surface. Her chair faced a window that had a soothing view of pine trees and distant mountains. "This is why you live up here."

"It is," she agreed. "I see deer and elk most times of the year. I could make more money other places" — she took another sip — "but I wouldn't have this kind of view. It's funny. I used to complain about the snow and icy roads when I lived in Denver. Even though the weather is harsher up here, I enjoy it now. It's peaceful."

The handwriting on the tab of a file folder caught his eye. DNM.com. His company. "What's this?"

"Something you weren't supposed to see yet," she said.

Her cheeks were so red they almost matched the colour of her wine. "Mind if I have a look?" he asked.

"Not at all."

While he flipped open the cover, she paced.

He found copies of each page of his website. Next he found pieces of paper with hand-drawn designs on them. The basic message was the same, but the look was more modern, fresh. Even his logo had been tweaked.

"Call me nosy. I was curious about you," she said, stopping next to the window, close enough that they could look at each other, but not close enough for him to touch her. "So I looked you up online."

He would have expected that. "Prudent in this day and age."

"No arrest records that I could find."

"Buried deep," he teased. "Records sealed."

"I'm good enough that I would have found something," she responded with appealing confidence. "I was impressed. You're involved with a number of different businesses."

"And some other things that could be added, or maybe a new one created."

"Your website doesn't appear to have been updated in the past few years. Your copyright is out of date and your SEO could use some fine tuning. You've got a few broken links. And I'm boring you."

"Not at all." In fact, the animation in her tone was infectious.

"I was going to give you some ideas to take to your web people. Sorry if I overstepped any bounds. Occupational hazard."

"Once you finish, I'll be interested in taking a look." He put down the folder, impressed by her resourcefulness and fresh eye. More and more, this woman appealed to him.

As he turned to leave the room, he noticed the wall behind her was decorated with pictures of dogs and cats. One had a photo of her with an older gentleman. They stood with their backs to a mountain, and they were each holding a trout. "Your father?"

She nodded. "Two summers ago near Shadow Mountain Lake."

"There's a strong resemblance."

"Especially the nose," she said, wrinkling hers.

"Nothing wrong with your nose."

"I'm delighted that you're blinded by lust, Sir."

He smacked her ass when she walked past him.

She yelped.

"One of my favourite sounds," he said.

Brandy continued the tour. "There's only one bathroom. But since it's just me, I manage fine."

It, too, fit the cottage theme with blue wainscoting and a claw-foot tub. A showerhead stuck out from the wall at a height designed for Brandy, rather than a man. "That's deep enough for two people."

"Is that a suggestion?"

"It could be."

A stackable washer and dryer stood in the far corner. Though small, the house had all the necessities.

"The other room is mine," she said.

And the door was closed. "Do you mind me seeing it?"

"I'm sure it's not your style." She shrugged. "But you probably intend to see it at some point."

"Only with your permission. But yes, I want to be in your bedroom."

"I was hoping you'd say that." She opened the door. "This, really, is why I bought this house."

"I would have, too." While the room wasn't large, its French doors made up for it. They opened onto a concrete patio that had a clay chimenea, two chairs and a small table. "You can watch the sunrise and have a cup of coffee?"

"I do, almost every day. In the summer, it can be hard to come back inside."

Her bed had at least nine pillows. Several were purple. The comforter was white. A white chaise longue sat at an angle perpendicular to the wall. A reading lamp drooped over the area, and a small table was next to it, a couple of books and an electronic reader stacked on the top. A fluffy pink throw was ultra-feminine, but fitting. A vase filled with wildflowers stood on top of a high dresser. The queen-size bed had a wooden headboard with lots of potential. "What's not to like about this room?"

"Some men find it threatens their masculinity."

"Some men?" he repeated, a sudden possessive urge stabbing at him.

"My dad and brother," she clarified right away. With a steady gaze, she met his eyes and added, "I don't have a lot of men in my bedroom, Sir, if that's what you're asking."

Good answer. He knew she was well within her rights to tell him to mind his own business or refuse to give him information. He appreciated that she hadn't made either of those choices. "Any man who is concerned by your décor hasn't thought about fucking you over the back of that chaise or tying your hair to the headboard."

She rolled the wine glass between her palms. "Is that what you're thinking?"

"That and propping those pillows beneath your stomach so that I can get your ass high enough to stuff my cock in it."

She stopped rolling the glass. "In that case, I won't change a single thing, Sir."

"The image will be that much hotter with my handprints already on your butt cheeks."

"All of a sudden, I'm thinking of cancelling the party."

"That's two of us."

She dropped her bra in a dresser drawer and closed it before he could get a proper look at all her lingerie.

"For later, Sir," she promised.

He followed her back to the kitchen and topped off her glass. He hadn't taken a sip from his. "How will you be introducing me tonight?"

"As Niles, an acquaintance I've known for a long time. I saw you at the grocery store and invited you."

"You took pity on a starving man," he added. "I'm another one of your strays."

She swept her gaze up his sexy body. "Do you think anyone will believe you're a stray?"

Outside, he heard a vehicle. So, too, did the dogs. Niles was almost ploughed over as they dashed towards the door.

"Party time," she said. She put down her glass and rubbed her ass. "Good thing I have on comfortable shoes, since I won't be able to sit down tonight."

"Perfect."

She flashed him a quick scowl before calling back the dogs and opening the door for the first of her visitors.

Over the next twenty minutes, at least a dozen people arrived, and no one asked about his relationship with Brandy. Though they seemed to all know one another, they included him in conversations and jokes. Beer flowed freely, and snacks of crudités and nuts vanished. A tall, thin woman stood near a table and tossed a candy-coated chocolate in her mouth every thirty seconds. Her coordination and timing were impressive.

The noise level steadily increased. Some guests moved into the living room, braver ones went outside with the beer and soft drinks, but most stayed in the kitchen.

He enjoyed watching her interact, moving from conversation to conversation with ease, calling out answers to questions from across the room, and opening beer bottles for others without being asked. She even glanced his direction a few times to make sure he was holding his own. Here or at the Den, Brandy was the perfect hostess. "It appears I should get the grill going," he said when she poured more candy into the dish.

"Good plan. Do you want matches or flamethrower, Sir?"

"Flamethrower," he said.

"Of course, Sir. It's in there." She pointed towards a drawer then grabbed the hamburgers from the refrigerator. "The cooking utensils and seasonings are already outside."

"You did a lot of preparation ahead of time."

"I wanted to have some free time in case you arrived early."

"I'm glad you did." Since there were other people around, he didn't continue the conversation. He cracked his knuckles then grabbed the long, thin lighter. "Show me the way."

He followed her through the carport and into the backyard.

The evening air was brisk. With the shorter days, it wouldn't be long before dusk descended.

She had set up a small table next to the grill, and she put the platter on top of it.

"Looks as if you thought of everything," he said, eyeing the extra plates, assorted spices and a long-handled spatula.

Brandy folded her arms across her chest as he lit the grill.

"What? Didn't think I was capable?" he asked.

"I just wanted to watch you work."

"Your nipples are hard."

"It's not just from the cold," she assured him.

"Anticipation?"

"And from remembering the night at the Den."

"I suppose we can't send everyone home until after we feed them?"

"No, Sir, we can't. But I'll be looking forward to the end of the evening." She excused herself, saying she needed to set out the garnishes and sliced cheese.

He watched her go. Within a few minutes, he started cooking the first burgers. It wasn't long before one of her male friends joined him.

"Need a hand?"

"John, isn't it?" Niles asked the tall, lanky man.

The man nodded and offered a beer.

"You're a friend for life," Niles said by way of thanks as he accepted the bottle of microbrew.

"So how did you meet Brandy?"

Niles answered with a question of his own, "Who are you to her?"

"Husband of her best friend." He shrugged.

"You drew the short straw? You had to be the one to check me out, see who I am, what my intentions are."

"Margot is curious. Brandy hasn't brought anyone to a party in a couple of years. And since she didn't say anything in advance, Margot's freaking out a bit. Those two share everything."

"I'm not a serial killer." Niles took a drink of the beer.

"So what do you do for a living?"

Niles looked at the man. He wondered if John had watched any of his videos, but then, what would it say about the man if he came right out and asked? Though he had a few businesses, Niles decided to find out how much John knew. "I own a video production company."

"Anything I might have seen?"

"You tell me." When John remained silent, but glanced away, Niles continued, "Does your wife know what you watch online?"

"Look, man…"

"Brandy is safe with me," he said.

Just then, she joined them. "How's it going?" She stopped and looked between the two of them.

Apparently sensing the tension, she levelled a look at John and asked, "Is Margot making you do her dirty work?"

Niles put down his drink and draped his arm across Brandy's shoulders, drawing her in close. She laid her head against his chest. It seemed natural, as if they'd done it a hundred times.

She felt warm and smelt of promise.

"Don't shoot the messenger," John pleaded.

"Not to worry," she said. "Master Niles only beats people who ask him nicely."

"Brandy," Niles warned, but he couldn't keep the mirth out of his tone. This tiny spitfire was ruffled on his behalf.

"I'm sorry, Sir, but I won't have you interrogated when you're a guest in my home."

He looked at her with a wry smile. She charmed him completely. "I'm the dragon, remember? I can take care of myself, Princess."

"I met him at a BDSM club," she told John, as if Niles hadn't spoken. "I've known him for a number of years," she added. "And this is not the first time he's defended my honour."

"You do realise that he —"

"For Christ's sake, John, yes. Please give me some credit."

Niles tightened his hold on her.

But that didn't slow her down. She said to John, "I'm curious how you know who he is." Then she gentled her voice. "Your job here is done, John," she continued. "I love you and Margot both, and I appreciate that you care. I'm going to tell Margot to come spend time with Master Niles and form her own opinion."

John raised his hands, defeated.

"I think the hamburgers are burning," she told them before squirming from Niles' grip and heading back inside.

"No hard feelings," John said.

"She's lucky to have friends like you," Niles responded.

John grabbed a plate and Niles transferred the meat onto it.

The man carried it inside while Niles put on the next batch.

Glad for a little solitude, he stood in front of the grill, drinking the last of his beer, watching the first tendrils of the orange sunset. He understood the appeal of this place for her. The views were spectacular.

The cabin he was staying at contained no personal effects. It had been decorated to appeal to hunters and fishermen, but with enough nicer touches that women didn't feel out of place. In contrast, she'd created a home. Dog toys were strewn about. And she had a greenhouse, with huge plants inside. He'd be hard-pressed to identify any of them, but he surmised it took a certain amount of attention to grow them that big. It was another outward sign of her nurturing personality.

Events like this, especially answering questions from nosy friends, wasn't his typical choice for an evening. Surprisingly, he was enjoying it.

Because he was still cooking, Brandy brought him a fresh beer along with a plate filled with potato salad, carrots, fruit and one of the charred burgers. He was grateful no one had criticised his barbecuing skills—at least not to his face.

The dogs spent a significant amount of time sitting near him—hoping to scavenge bits of meat, he was sure. He glanced around, looking for Brandy before splitting an overdone patty in half and feeding it to the animals.

"That's one way to stop MW from biting your feet," John observed, bringing out another beer for Niles. "I was sent to light the chimenea. Penance for pissing off both women."

"Tough times," Niles agreed.

"I'm curious. What's it like being around so many beautiful women all the time?"

He didn't have to think about his answer. "Unrewarding. Meaningless."

"Seriously, man?"

"Be grateful for what you have."

"Sounds as if you're part philosopher."

Niles took a drink of beer. "Just wish I had appreciated things more when I had the chance."

John grabbed the flamethrower and set about lighting the small chimenea fire while Niles, his duties over, turned off the grill.

The warmth and glow drew a small crowd, and he was soon engaged in conversations with people who had a much different approach to life than he did. He chatted with a ski instructor who worked only a few months a year, a fly fishing guide and a stay-at-home father. Margot and John ran a small breakfast restaurant in Grand Lake, so they were amongst the first to leave, but Margot narrowed her gaze at Niles in a silent reminder that she wasn't certain about his intentions.

Now, as Brandy said goodbye to the last of her guests, he made sure the fire was out before going inside and tackling the arduous task of loading the dishwasher. Even when it was full, the counters and table top were still messy. The contrast between her kitchen and his pristine one startled him. It made him see how empty and solitary his life had become since he'd lost Eleanor.

Back then, he and his wife had enjoyed a whirlwind social life. She'd been a prominent attorney, he'd been an investment broker, and they'd been aware of the need to network their way to success.

When they had entertained, Eleanor had hired caterers. He'd never had to deal with an aftermath like this.

"Did I scare you off?" she asked, coming back inside. She flipped the switch to turn off the outdoor lights.

"Despite the gnawing terror, I'm still here," he said.

"That's right. After all, you are a big, bad, brave Dom. You didn't need to pitch in. But thank you. I'll handle the rest of the clean-up in the morning." She propped her hips against a cupboard and looked at him.

Even though there'd been plenty of noise and mayhem with the pets and the party, he was amazed by how relaxed he felt.

"I hope you enjoyed it, at least a little. You did great on the burgers."

"They were burnt."

"Which is better than raw," she pointed out.

"Are you always an optimist?"

"Guilty."

"And yeah. I did enjoy myself." He took the last sip from his beer. "Even though you didn't need me."

"Of course I needed you, Sir."

"I think John could have handled it. He owns a restaurant."

She had the good grace to flush a bit. "I like to give him the night off if he comes here. The guy who does most of the cooking really is out of town."

"Fair enough." He believed her. She would think about her friends and how they deserved the chance to rest. It endeared her to him even more. "Where's the soap?"

"Why?"

"So we can wash the rest of these dishes."

"Really, Sir. Thank you, but you've helped enough."

Her tone was abrupt, and a scowl was wedged between her eyebrows. Keeping his tone light, he asked, "Do you refuse everyone's help?"

"Not at all."

"Then it's me."

"It's not..." She sucked in a breath. "Well, yes, it is you. You're a Dom."

"Doms can't wash dishes? They need to put up their feet and have a cocktail while you do all the housework and come to bed exhausted? For good measure you could be scolded for not moving faster and rubbing my feet?"

"Sounds ridiculous when you say it like that."

"It is ridiculous," he agreed. "I want to get you naked."

"Stop." Her scowl deepened.

"I've made you uncomfortable. Tell me why."

When she remained silent, he added, "I've somehow blundered into an emotional limit, and I'd like to understand it." He wasn't sure what in the hell had happened in the last few minutes, but God damn if he'd let it go.

"I think it means something if you help me with chores."

"It only has the meaning you give it. Can you accept help from a friend?"

She sighed. "People in a relationship help each other with dishes."

"Ah. So if I help you, I have to move in? Or maybe I drag you to Denver and force you to make my dinner?"

She laughed, scattering the tension. "You're being outrageous."

"Am I?" He looped his arms around her waist and drew her close. "I hear nervousness in your voice, but it's okay for us to relax around each other. And to be honest, I'd prefer to deal with this tonight instead of facing it in the morning before I've had my coffee."

"So that means you're spending the night?"

Her words had a hesitation, a brief skip that seemed at odds with the confident persona he'd seen from her so far. He was seeing the real Brandy, rather than the personality she presented in public. He folded his arms across his chest. "I apologise. I shouldn't be presumptuous. I'd like to, but I'll leave the choice to you," he said. His body responded to hers the way it did every time they stood close. He'd be a gentleman if she wanted him to be, but his cock was voting in favour of her asking him to stay.

Chapter Four

Deep inside, nerves and anticipation collided, merged, then arrowed up Brandy's spine.

All day, she'd been thinking about this moment. When he'd accepted her invitation to the party, she'd hoped he would stay. It had been difficult to keep moving forward with preparations when all she'd wanted to do was indulge in adult-themed fantasises.

Still, now that the moment was here, she realised this was a monumental step. Not for him, she was sure, but for her. Master Niles was a self-assured Dom whose resources allowed him to have a different woman every day of the week if he wanted.

On this small plot of mountain land, she'd created a sanctuary. She'd invited no one to share it with her.

She'd thought she could have him over, have a scene and be casual the next morning, but she was finding out it wasn't so easy for her.

Master Niles was more complex than she'd believed him to be from their few meetings at the Den. If she were honest, she would admit that part of her had been surprised when he'd shown up prepared to grill.

His barbecue skills were only a few steps above dismal. He seemed to give people two choices in how they liked their burgers cooked — burnt or charred. Still, he'd shocked her by seeming at ease. He'd had 'a couple of beers, rather than expensive cocktails, and when she'd checked on him through the windows, he'd been engaged in conversation. By the end of the evening, he'd shaken John's hand. Brandy liked that Master Niles didn't scare easily.

But wanting to work together after her guests had left...that took the relationship to a new, uncomfortable level.

He'd made light of her observation that he wasn't behaving like a Dom. If he'd stay within the lines of her preconceived boundaries, things would be easier for her. She wore submission like a comfortable blanket. It kept her warm and safe. But taking it off revealed the real, vulnerable person beneath. She'd vowed to keep that person hidden and protected.

Master Niles continued to say nothing, and he eased away from her, giving her space. He took the last drink from his beer then slid the empty bottle onto the countertop.

His words still hung between them, ripe with expectation.

Why the hell had he gone and complicated things?

He didn't rush her decision, and she appreciated that he would respect anything she decided. She knew she was flirting with danger. Despite that, she wanted to be back in his arms. If he left, the loneliness would be worse than the potential emotional risk. "I'd like you to stay."

He captured her hand and raised it to his lips with old-world elegance. "My pleasure," he said.

With his touch, awareness skittered across her nerve endings. Oh *yes*. She'd made the right decision. Her imagination provided half a dozen scenarios for what they might do later, and each image was more evocative than the previous one.

"Now, about your refusal of my help with the dishes…" He released her and grabbed a hand towel. With focused intent, he made small circles with his wrist, wrapping the towel round and round.

"Oh no you don't," she said, dancing a few steps away from him. She never knew what to expect from him, from playful and teasing to thoughtful and kind and back again. "That's for high school boys in a locker room."

"It's also for subs who argue with their Doms."

"No, no!" Her gaze was riveted on his hand. She wanted him to smack her with the whirling towel. Alternately, she knew it would hurt. Most of all, she wanted this light moment to continue and chase away her fears. "Come on, Master Niles, I was trying to be a good sub. I wanted you to relax like you deserve. I was being nice to you."

"Uh-huh." He took a deliberate step towards her.

"That'll burn like a bitch."

"Take it like a woman."

"I don't want to!" She squealed in mock terror.

The dogs danced around and barked as he drew back his hand. He continued to swirl the fabric.

"Present your ass, sub."

"I promise to make you work like a hired hand next time you're here. I'll even let you put away all the leftovers by yourself. You can scrub the floors if you want. With a toothbrush. I'll sit and watch television while you do it. Promise."

"This will hurt more if I make you remove your skirt."

"Oh fine. Hit me with your best shot." With a saucy grin, she turned her backside to him and flicked her ponytail. She intended to skitter out of his reach by the time he let the towel fly. But his speed stunned her. He flicked his wrist, catching her bottom in a searing strike. "Yowzer!"

"Now can we clean the kitchen, or would you like to argue some more?"

Turning to face him, she rubbed the sting. "Damn, Sir, you don't show any mercy."

"Do you want me to?"

Did she? Their gazes locked.

"I want what you're offering," she confessed.

"Good. Me, too." He tossed the towel towards the counter, but Dana snatched it from mid-air and hurried off to her crate. "You were right. She is fast. Sorry about that."

MW's nails scrabbled on the tiled floor as he struggled to keep up so he could nip the larger dog's heels.

"I'll get it later. If I try to get it now, she'll think we are playing tug-of-war."

When they ignored the animals, they settled down.

"Get to work," he instructed. He raised an eyebrow. "Unless you want another spanking."

"Sorry, Sir, was that supposed to be motivation?"

"I could withhold one for the next few weeks."

"Anything but that," she protested as she bent to grab the dish soap from beneath the sink. She didn't miss the fact he was speaking in terms of seeing each other in the future or the fact his eyes no longer seemed shadowed by pain.

Fifteen minutes later, he closed the last cupboard door. Every surface had been washed and dried. Even the floor had been swept.

"Now…" he said, reaching for her and drawing her near like he had earlier.

She settled into his arms with alarming ease.

"Getting that finished wasn't so bad. Was it?"

"You were right, Sir."

"My favourite words," he said.

"Of course they are." Brandy wound her hands around his neck. For this moment, it was as if they were new lovers as well as submissive and Dominant. His cock pressed against her, and her pussy moistened in immediate response.

When he narrowed his eyes, putting all his focus solely on her, her knees weakened. She leaned against him more and dug her fingers into his hair. "Want," she murmured.

Brandy had thought she'd been prepared… He claimed her mouth with deliberation mixed with longing. His tongue brushed hers in a gentle tease rather than the intensity she'd expected.

He tasted of beer with a faint undertone of chocolate. She hadn't known he had a sweet tooth.

With slow, measured precision, he deepened the kiss. Her body came to life.

Her Dom opened his mouth wider and demanded deeper access. Then he splayed a hand across her buttocks and brought her in even closer. She met him with fire rather than submissive inevitability.

He was muscle and sinew and relentless male energy. He moved his other hand to her upper back and applied enough pressure to smash her breasts again his chest. Every breath she took was stamped by his masculine essence.

Deftly, he manoeuvred them so that he could grab the hem of her sweater and pull it over her head.

He looked at her bared torso. Her breasts felt heavy, and her nipples ached for his attention.

"Making you go braless was a bad decision."

Her skin heated beneath his smouldering approval. "Was it, Sir?"

"Torture," he added.

"For me, too."

"Oh?"

"You pinched my nipples earlier, and all night, my sweater rubbed me, keeping them hard. Then when I saw you looking at me…"

"I wanted to have you up against the back of the house when you came outside the first time, all avenging angel to protect me from John. An angel with the nipples of a siren. I should punish you for making me have a hard-on all night."

"Serves you right, Sir. I was just being a good sub and doing what you said." His swift responses when she was sassy should have already taught her to hold her tongue, but she couldn't resist.

"I'm going to put you in a full girdle. One that hides your breasts."

"You could just keep your magnificent libido in check," she teased.

"And that's how I intend to do it. Unless you want to find yourself ravished even if you have a houseful of guests."

"Ravished, Sir?"

He shrugged. "Sounds better than being banged."

"Either word is perfect, as long as it's not just talk." She continued, even though she knew it was risky, "Back it up with some action, Sir."

He tossed the sweater on top of a cupboard. MW leapt up. Master Niles didn't say a word. Instead, he levelled a look at the dog. With a soft whine, MW plopped back down.

"How do you do that?" she asked.

"It's about force of will," he said.

"Ah. I see."

"It's inevitable. No need to fight it." He dropped a kiss on the top of her head.

The intimate gesture made her feel cared for.

"Do we need to do anything with the dogs before bed?"

"I don't make them sleep in their crates. Most times they prefer to, but I don't lock them in."

"If I remember correctly, your bedroom has a door?"

"It does. No need to worry that your toes will get bitten while we're in bed."

As if he were reluctant to let her go, he released her by slow measures. It took her just as long to drop her arms to her sides.

"Would you like a shower first, Sir?"

"I'd like to fuck you, then shower, then fuck you again." His eyes were dark, mysterious. "By then, you might be warmed up."

Brandy gulped. She didn't know him well enough to know if he was joking, but she suspected he wasn't.

Though they'd stepped apart, sexual tension vibrated in the atmosphere, promising to reignite.

"Is everything locked up?"

"I wanted to double-check the front door. Someone may have gone out that way."

He nodded then handled the task. It was small, menial yet it mattered a great deal to her. She'd spent so long taking care of herself that having someone else ease part of the load seemed huge.

In a way it frightened her. If she came to count on him, she would be setting herself up for failure. But how could she do otherwise when his personality loomed so big?

In a surprise move, one that affirmed the nature of their relationship, he came back to cup her head with his palm. To outsiders, this would never look out of place, but it showed her that Dominance wasn't an occasional thing to him. It was an extension of his alpha personality. She shivered.

"Cold?"

"No, Sir," she whispered, meeting his all-seeing gaze.

"Then you're responding to me."

"Yes..."

He tightened his grip, and she closed her eyes in submissive bliss. Her whole life, she'd craved this kind of intimacy. She'd had plenty of relationships, some with Doms, some with men who tried to give her what she wanted, some with vanilla guys who had no interest in helping her get her kink on.

This, however, was delicious because of its naturalness.

Master Niles couldn't help being who he was, and she was powerless to do anything other than respond to his masculine resolve.

He drew her head back, and she looked at him.

His strong jaw was set in a tight line. His features were inscrutable. She reminded herself she didn't know much about him. Gregorio had warned her not to get her heart broken. His words echoed in her mind as if he were standing there.

She couldn't allow herself to get swept up in the moment with Master Niles and begin to think this meant anything to him. He'd used the word friend and dispelled her earlier fears. They were two consenting adults enjoying each other's company, nothing more. No matter how devastatingly handsome he was.

"Shall we get on with the ravishing?" he asked.

The darkness in his eyes had vanished. "Or the banging," she added, responding in kind.

He kept his hand in place as he led her to the bedroom and closed the door.

Without a word, he lowered her to her knees. *So, so right.* When he dropped his hands, she missed his touch. But with trained patience, she waited for him to speak.

"Is there anything we need to discuss, Brandy?"

They needed to get this out of the way, and she appreciated him taking time for it, even though she was anxious to feel him inside her. "If it suits you, Sir, we can use the Den's protocols. Halt for a safe word. Safe limits, nothing that will cause permanent scarring and, of course, we'll use condoms. There are some in the nightstand drawer."

He nodded.

The necessities out of the way, she glanced at the floor, using the motion to ground herself in a submissive mind-set. "May I help you with your boots, Sir?"

"Please do."

His instruction was firm, not a request, but an order. The command in his tone settled her as effectively as a touch, and she drank it like the finest wine.

Brandy untied the laces. He sat on the mattress while she removed his hiking boots then slid them next to a pair of her sandals beneath the bed.

"Thank you," he said, after she'd tucked his socks away.

A lot of subs she knew didn't embrace small acts of servitude with the reverence she did. Something about making her Dom's life somewhat easier fed her soul. She enjoyed all the physical acts as well—beatings, bondage—but to her, submission was an entire package. And as she'd explained to friends and family who weren't in the lifestyle, her preferences didn't make her a doormat. Domination and submission were symbiotic. Things needed to be in balance for success.

He'd cooked, helped with the clean-up, entertained her guests and made certain the house was secure.

"Finish stripping for me. I want to see the rest of your body naked. You may stand."

They'd been together before, and recently he'd spanked her. She shouldn't feel anxious, but with him sitting there on her bed, arms folded across his chest, she did. She wanted to please him.

She rose and wriggled out of her skirt. Right now she wished she'd worn stockings instead of tights, but he'd expressed no displeasure. Earlier, he'd used them to all but hobble her.

"Nice."

Their gazes met. His voice held heat. He was obviously not disappointed in her choice.

Emboldened by that knowledge, she decided to do a bit of a striptease.

She toed off her sheepskin-lined boots then crouched to tuck them beneath the bed, not far from his legs.

"Brandy…"

"Sir?" It took all her concentration not to grin. Of course she knew she held the power, but she also recognised how fleeting it was. He could and would snatch it back in an instant.

She did a little hip wiggle as she stood. Then, turning her back to him, she slid her fingers beneath the tight elastic band and started to shimmy the material down her legs.

"Stop."

She froze. The sound of his voice brooked no refusal. He scared her, thrilled her. Like earlier, her tights were around her knees, and she was effectively hobbled.

"Grab your ankles."

Damn, she loved the carnality of a D/s relationship. No vanilla guy had ever ordered her around like this. Never knowing what to expect thrilled her.

Once she was in position, he stood. Upside down, she remained where she was, struggling to remember to breathe.

He walked around her slowly, looking at her. After stopping behind her, he pulled down her thong and slid a finger between the plump folds of her pussy. Her clit throbbed.

"So beautiful," he said.

Master Niles stroked faster, and she moved her hips, seeking more. This afternoon, he'd allowed her to hump his leg, and she was all but doing the same thing to his hand now.

"I should take a picture of your pretty little cunt."

"Anything you say, Sir." As long as he let her get off.

"You're getting wetter."

"I am..."

He stroked faster.

"Oh, Master Niles!"

"That's it, gorgeous sub. You can come now or you can wait. Your choice."

"I'm not certain I understand, Sir." She was delirious, lost. Her hair spilled everywhere, and she closed her eyes as the first tendrils claimed her. She was on the verge of satisfaction or painful denial.

"If you come now, I'll punish you for it, and it will be the only one you get. If you wait, you'll have as many orgasms as you want later."

Her body shook.

He didn't ask again. Instead he kept stroking her with the same rhythm and pressure. The more he touched her the quicker she started to unravel. She tried to swim through the haze of sensation. Delay the sensation? Or grab the release that was right there, even if it meant dealing with more of this unrequited tension later? "Whatever you prefer, Sir." She curled her toes under, trying to hold on.

He didn't answer.

"Sir, Sir, Sir!" She gulped in gasps of air.

"Wait. I want you to fight it off."

She exhaled a shaky gasp, relieved that he'd made the decision. But instead of removing his hand, the heartless bastard kept up his ministrations. "Oh, fuck!"

"I won't think less of you if you disobey me."

She pulled away from him a bit, but her body's needs betrayed her. Like a hussy, she swayed, moving her hips back. "You'll punish me, though."

"Of course I will."

"Then..." Thoughts tumbled. "I'm begging you..." How could he know what she wanted when she couldn't decide? She hadn't been with him enough to know how he meted out punishment. Perhaps they were even better than this. "Please." *Please, yes. Please, no.* "I'm going to..."

"What are you asking for, Brandy?"

The orgasm was right *there*. In the end, she was too much of a sub to truly want to disregard his decision. "Stop touching me, Sir."

"Anything you wish." He eased his hand away.

It was as if dozens of pins danced across her skin, sensitising her. She rose up then slammed her heels down as she struggled to come back from the edge. Being upside down kept her disoriented, and she felt alternately chilled and overheated.

"Are you forgetting something?"

"Oh, God." Breath threatened to choke her. "Thank you for stopping, Sir."

He began to touch her again.

She swam in a pool of confusion. "Sir?"

"Offering a little reinforcement of my desire to always hear you use your manners," he informed her.

Now she had her answer to her earlier question. Master Niles was creative and diabolical about his punishments. She felt lightheaded from being bent over for so long. Her pussy was slippery. He quickened his strokes, and the intensity of the pinpricks quadrupled. "I apologise, Sir. I know to be grateful for your kindness. Thank you."

"Apology accepted."

She sighed with relief. But he never paused. "Sir?" The sound of her heart echoed in her ears.

"As I said, I'm ensuring you learn the lesson."

"Oh, Sir, I'm a fast learner."

"What are you not going to do?"

"I'm not going to come, Sir."

"What are you going to do?"

"Use my manners, Sir."

Other exacting Doms had spanked her for her rare lapses, but she knew this unique form of torture would linger.

He tweaked her labia then pushed his thumb against her clit. She jerked away from his hand but forced herself back into position before he needed to correct her laxness. "Edge, Sir," she told him, letting him know she was on the verge.

It was as if she hadn't spoken.

"Thank you for the lesson," she said. "I'm finding it very instructive." She was babbling to distract herself from the power of the approaching orgasm.

"There are ways for me to keep you right where you are without letting you come, heightening your tension for minutes, maybe an hour."

"This isn't it, is it, Sir?"

"Smart sub."

In fact, she suspected his touch was calculated to force her orgasm, not stall it.

"You're diabolical, Sir. And I'm grateful."

He laughed and the warm, genuine sound drenched her in intimacy.

"Very grateful." Her clit seemed to have swollen to twice its normal size, and she felt him pull back its little hood, exposing more of it. She dug her fingernails into her ankles. Her tights constricted her movements, and she couldn't part her legs to dissipate the tingling.

Unable to decide what to do, out of viable techniques, she surrendered and tried to let her mind float. "Thank you," she murmured. If she couldn't hold on, if he won this battle, at least she would have a shattering orgasm out of it. "Thank you," she repeated. Not just for the lesson, but for the attention, the way he noted her reactions and his relentlessness. "Thank you." Over and over, she repeated the words until they became part blur, part mantra. Somewhere, she forgot about herself. A moment ago, she'd been thinking about her own satisfaction. Now, with startling insight, she knew nothing was more important than pleasing him.

She shut out everything else but thoughts of him.

"That's it. Fight it because your Dom demands it of you."

His voice seemed to drift in from a long way off. *Her Dom.* Time and space fractured.

"Good girl."

His voice penetrated her foggy thoughts, and she realised he'd been talking to her for some time. Along the way, he'd stopped touching her and she hadn't been aware of it. By slow measures she noticed her surroundings, her throbbing pussy and the sensation of peace that cloaked her.

Transcending her needs to satisfy her Dom's command gave her a sense of satisfied bliss. This feeling didn't happen to her often, and she lived for the moments it did. "Thank you," she whispered a final time as she opened her eyes.

"You're magnificent," he said as he crouched behind her.

She saw his face, its power, the determined set of his jaw. She wondered if he ever allowed himself to relax.

"Open your mouth."

When she did, he slipped his fingers inside.

"Clean them."

She licked. The combination of his skin and her tangy taste deepened their sense of connection. This man was so, so sexy. At the Den, his actions had been about her pleasure as much as—if not more than—his own. Tonight he seemed to have the same intention. Many Doms she played with would have had her on her knees already, pumping their dicks into her mouth as if racing to an invisible finish line. But he seemed to want to savour every moment.

"Good," he said.

He extracted his fingers then grabbed her around the hips to steady her. "I'll help you up."

"I'd appreciate that, Sir. Thank you. I'm not sure I can stand under my own power."

Shocking her, he swept her from her feet and deposited her on the bed.

"Tights," he said, "the most underrated form of bondage. Maybe I'll take you out in public with the waistband around your thighs."

"I'm sure I'd look like a duck rather than a seductress, Sir."

"Regardless, you'd be very much aware of your place."

"Sir, any woman, whether she's into the lifestyle or not, is going to be aware of her place around you."

"I'm not interested in any other woman."

The force in his words made her slide back on the bed.

Legs planted far apart, arms folded across his chest, he added, "We're talking about you, Brandy."

She chose her next words with great care. "Sir, from the moment I saw you at the Den two years ago, I've known who you are. And I'm not talking about your name or reputation. You have a way of moving, speaking, behaving that makes me very much aware of being female and reinforces my submissiveness. It doesn't matter if I am naked and chained at your feet, or dressed in that girdle you threatened me with —"

"I assure you, it wasn't merely a threat."

Breath whooshed from her lungs. His enigmatic remoteness both thrilled and frightened her. "No matter where we are, Sir, whether we're out in public, or surrounded by my friends, I could never deny the force of your personality, nor would I want to. That you are a Dom excites me. I've thought about you since the evening we scened together." Lowering her voice, she confessed, "I've masturbated to the memory."

"Have you?"

"Yes."

"Show me."

"Sir?"

"Masturbate. Tell me what you were thinking while you were doing it."

The suggestion energised her.

With quick and efficient movements, he finished undressing her before tossing her clothing on the floor.

"I'll need my vibrator," she said.

"Where is it?"

"Bottom dresser drawer. Left side. Under my jeans."

"Hiding it from company?"

"My version of a quick clean up before guests started to arrive," she confessed, hoping he had no need to go into her closet. All the mess from her office had been piled in there.

She propped a pillow behind her head and asked, "Will you also grab a pair of my nipple clamps, Sir?"

"You have several. Any preference?"

"The tweezers, please."

He returned to the bedside a moment later and plugged in the massager before offering the clamps.

"Would you like to put them on me, Sir?"

"Did you use them when you thought of me?"

"I did," she admitted.

"In that case, I want to watch."

She accepted the sturdy metal chain that he offered. For both of them, this was unique. In his videos, he competently dominated the models and actresses. When she scened with men — Master Niles included — they took control.

He loomed over her. Excited anticipation made her mouth dry.

"Pretend I'm not here."

"You know that's impossible, Sir." Hyperaware of his stance and his stare, she tried to shut him out and follow his instructions.

She placed a pillow beneath her knees and spread her legs before closing her eyes and squeezing her left breast.

"You like more pressure than I knew," he said.

"I do." She toyed with her nipple, playing at first to get it hard. Then she twisted it. She arched her back in pleasure. "Even before I affixed the first clamp the other night, I was remembering our time together at the Den, the way you told me to cut the bullshit." She pulled on her nipple, distending it.

She opened her eyes so that she could see where she was placing the rubber tips.

"You're giving me an idea for a new script," he said.

There was a husky tone in his voice that made goosebumps skitter down her spine. "As I slid this part up" — she took hold of the small piece of metal that tightened the clamps — "I was recalling how nervous that made me, as if you saw through the act I sometimes bring to my job. You scared me a little, Sir, but that thrilled me, too. I've been wanting a man who will demand more than I usually give."

Brandy met his gaze.

His eyes were narrowed, and he'd moved a bit closer to her. He was looking at her as if she were the only woman on the planet who mattered. Was it any wonder she fantasised about him?

"May I?" he asked as she reached to fondle her right breast.

"Please," she murmured.

He took hold of her flesh with some tenderness, but when he tightened his grip, her pussy moistened.

"Damn, Sir," she said when he readjusted his grip and simply rolled her nipple between his thumb and forefinger. "Nice."

"Thought you might appreciate that amount of pressure."

She couldn't string two coherent thoughts together.

He let go of her and placed the clamp, sliding the clip into place. "Like this?" he asked.

There was the same tension on both nipples. "You follow examples well, Sir."

"I'm watching you," he told her. "Every movement."

"Were you always a straight A student?"

"In the subjects that mattered to me." He moved away. "Go on," he encouraged.

"Then I thought about the way you fingered me." She pulled back the hood of her clitoris and stroked the tiny nub.

He nodded. "It's lovely. So swollen already."

Brandy picked up the vibrator with its overly large head and turned on the power switch to the lowest setting. With him watching her, she'd be shattering in less than thirty seconds if she flipped it on high.

"Talk to me," he reminded her.

"When I put this against my pussy, I was remembering the way you told me you owed me a punishment for coming without permission even though you forced it from me."

"I hadn't forgotten."

She turned her head.

"You're not the only one who's been thinking about it," he said.

"But I was sure that was just part of the scene…"

"I keep my promises, and I remember what I say. I would have searched you out and held you accountable the next time I saw you at the Den."

She looked away from him. Her memories and his words drove her response. "When I masturbated before, it was good, Sir, but nothing like this." She dug her heels into the mattress and lifted her pelvis. "You fingered me."

"I remember."

"And you ate my cunt."

"A part of your body that needs more attention, I'm sure."

"Yes, Sir." Her thighs trembled. Knowing he was here, enjoying himself, increased the sensuality of the experience.

"Watching you is so fucking hot, Brandy."

"It's you, Sir…"

"How long did it take you to come?"

"About two minutes, Sir."

"See if you can last that long this time."

"Sir, I'm always in trouble for coming too soon," she said miserably.

"I'll make it worth your while to wait."

As she writhed, losing herself in memories and fighting back the impending orgasm, the bastard flipped the switch to high. Brandy moaned. At every turn, he challenged her. She'd known dozens of Doms, and none were as diabolical as Master Niles.

"That's a good girl," he said. "Less than a minute to go."

Presuming she didn't lose her mind first.

She mentally counted backwards from sixty.

Out of her peripheral vision, she saw him remove the rest of his clothes. Thank God. She sensed, rather than saw, him open the nightstand and take out a condom.

"Before you came, what were you thinking about?"

"What?" She concentrated. At first his question made no sense, but then it clicked. "What made me come was recalling the way the flogger felt on my body."

He turned off the vibrator and pulled it away, leaving her shaking with need. The sudden silence and lack of stimulation shocked her.

Before she could ask any questions, he knelt on the bed between her legs.

"Open your mouth."

She complied, and he put the metal chain from the clamps between her teeth.

He grabbed her ankles and lifted her hips from the pillow, looking at her pussy and simultaneously preventing her from moving. He kept her like that for a long while. He was preventing her orgasm and yet keeping her aroused.

"Put your legs on my shoulders."

Which meant...

He licked her pussy.

Double damn, he was good at that. She closed her eyes in surrender. It only took a few moments for her to get close again.

Having the chain to the clamps in her mouth kept her quiet and still. Her nipples were already a bit sore, and she didn't want to make them feel worse.

She dug her hands into his hair, bringing his head closer. He responded to her unspoken request by sucking and sliding a finger inside her. She was lost.

"Come for me, sub."

Her thrashing yanked on her nipple clamps, magnifying the pain and shooting arrows of awareness towards her pussy.

With a muffled cry, she came.

He kept at it, licking, sucking, finger-fucking, forcing her to ride the high for longer than she'd known possible.

This Dom knew how to read her body.

When she screamed out, she released the chain from her mouth. She shook her head, trying to clear the myriad colours and thoughts that clouded her mind. She'd never had sex like this. Though this didn't have all the trappings of a BDSM scene, there was no doubt he was in control, and she loved it. "Sir, that was…"

"You taste delicious. I need to start you out like that every time."

"Thank you, Sir." A thrill lanced her. He was a generous lover. She was more relaxed than she ever remembered being. And that she could fall asleep after this was over, rather than driving home, made it a hundred times better.

Master Niles was everything she'd ever wanted in a Dominant, and this was everything she'd dreamt of having in a love affair. She knew she'd be a fool to think it was anything more than a one-evening kick. In the morning he'd go home. Brandy told herself to relax into the moment and enjoy it, rather than worrying about the loss she'd feel when her bed and her life were empty again.

"Hands above your head, sub."

It took her several seconds to obey. The backs of her thighs burned, and the rest of her body felt lethargic.

"I'm not done with you."

She wondered if his words were a promise or a threat.

He gave one of her buttocks a sharp smack. "Threat," she said with a gasp as she followed his order.

"Sorry?" he asked.

"I was wondering if your statement was a promise or a threat," she said.

"I don't say things I don't mean, Ms Hess."

"Clearly, Sir."

He grinned and she smiled back, a momentary, sexy connection.

Master Niles positioned himself at her entrance, and he kept her legs high. As he eased into her, the backs of her thighs were stretched tight.

"Ready?"

"Yes, Sir. Fuck me."

In a long stroke, he sank into her. She gasped from the shock of the force. "Yes," she said when she was able to breathe again.

He stayed still for a few seconds as she accommodated his length.

"That's it, my gorgeous sub."

In response to his approval, she clenched her internal muscles, trying to draw him deeper.

"Squeeze my cock."

Her body felt as if it were made for his searing penetration. Using the leverage of his shoulders, she lifted her hips, meeting his thrusts and tightening her muscles around his penis. "So hot, Sir. So deep."

"Perfect," he agreed.

He captured her wrists in one of his strong hands. Everything about him was delicious. And the added bite of the clamps heightened everything even more.

He knew exactly how to arouse her. "Sir, I need to come again."

"Do," he encouraged, shortening his strokes, but going deeper.

Perspiration drenched her. "Do me, Sir!"

He pounded into her the way she wanted.

"Yeah, this is what you need."

"Yes, Sir. It is. It is!" She drew the 's' out until it became half sigh, half scream.

He tightened his grip on her wrists and ordered, "Come."

Jerking against him, helpless, she did. He continued to fuck her, drawing out her orgasm, making her ride it longer than she imagined possible.

Finally, replete, she let her body go slack.

"That will do for a warm-up."

"Warm-up, Sir?" She cleared her throat. "I'm not certain I'll survive whatever else you have in mind."

"I'll make sure you do." He withdrew his still-hard cock and left the bed.

Confusion chased away her sense of satisfaction. "Sir?" From his absence, mentally and physically, she shivered.

"I promised you a shower."

"But you didn't..."

"I'll get mine, Brandy. Up," he told her.

"I don't think I can move." Not that she wanted to. "You've got a magnificent body, Sir." His cock thrust forward. She rolled to one side and propped her head on her hand to get a better look at him as he removed the condom and discarded it in a trash can.

Damn, she appreciated his trim hips and lean torso. His powerful legs and cut biceps spoke of raw strength. Despite feeling satiated, a primal beat pulsed in her, reawakening her sexual interest.

"I told you to get up," he repeated, folding his arms across his chest.

When she didn't immediately move, he did.

He grabbed her from the bed then tossed her over his shoulder. She flailed and kicked, and he swatted her bare butt—hard.

"Ow, Sir!"

"Next time, do as you're told, when you're told."

He strode out of the bedroom, jostling her as he walked.

"Your shoulder is knobby," she complained.

"Poor thing."

Blood rushed to her head and the ground swayed beneath her. And there was no place she'd rather be than this close to him. She braced her palms on his back.

In the bathroom he deposited her on the countertop.

"That's cold, Sir," she said.

"My apologies, Princess. Maybe you'd be more comfortable on your knees?"

She yielded to the impulse to link her hands around his neck. "If you say so, Sir."

"I do." His motions at odds with the simmering passion in his eyes, he placed her on the tile floor before putting a hand on her head and forcing her down.

His dick filled her vision.

"Lick it. No hands."

"I love the way you taste," she said before placing her tongue against the underneath of his cockhead. She did as he'd said then she sucked him into her mouth.

"I said to lick it, sub."

His tone held a sexy growl that drove her mad. Mindful of his order, she let his cock slip from her mouth before angling her head to lick his shaft from slit to balls.

"That's better," he said.

He might be a big, bad, demanding Dom, but the way he dug his hands into her hair and held her assured her he appreciated her.

He grew thicker, and she knew he had to be close to ejaculating when he moved away from her. "Kneel back."

"Yes, Sir."

"You could say that like you mean it."

"I'm too well trained to tell you what I really thought, Sir."

"You'll get as much cock as you want later, sub."

Satisfaction oozed through her.

He turned on the water and adjusted the temperature then extended his hand.

She accepted and allowed him to draw her up. "I need to put my hair up." She grabbed two large clips from a basket beneath the sink.

"Allow me." He plucked one of the plastic pieces from her palm and scooped up a handful of strands. He inhaled the scent. "Peach?" he asked.

"With vanilla." No man had ever done something she found so exotically appealing.

"I like it."

She made a note to buy a dozen bottles on her next trip into town.

Within moments, he had secured her hair. "I could play with this for hours."

"I'd let you, Sir."

He pulled back the shower curtain and entered the tub. "Join me?" he invited.

She'd always thought the tub was one of the home's nicest features. Its claw feet reminded her of a bygone era, and its depth allowed her to soak up to her chin, something divine in winter when the house was cold.

Although her father had added a showerhead during the remodel, she hadn't noticed how small the tub was for two people to stand in. Until now. She couldn't be more than a foot away from Master Niles. This close, his presence overwhelmed her.

"Not too hot?" he asked when they were beneath the spray with the shower curtain pulled closed.

"It's perfect, Sir." Just like the rest of the evening had been. "May I wash your back?"

"Please." He turned away from her.

"Damn, you're every bit as hot from this angle, Master Niles." She made lazy circles on his back.

Steam billowed around them, and she squatted to make her way down and across his tight buttocks. She gently slid into the crack to cleanse him there.

His body went rigid, and she continued down his legs. "I've showered with men before," she admitted. "But I've never washed their backs."

"Your Doms have been remiss," he said. "If you were mine, bathing me would be a Friday night obligation."

"One I'd enjoy, Sir." The experience of combining service and sensuality would be sublime. "Did your wife do that for you, Sir?"

His one word answer was flat. "No."

Wondering if she was being reckless, she persisted. "Would you have liked her to?"

He didn't reply.

Brandy knew she didn't have the right to push for an answer, but curiosity made her hold her tongue as the question hung in the atmosphere while she continued the soothing ministrations across his already-clean skin.

When she was certain he didn't intend to respond, he said, "It never occurred to me to make it a requirement."

"I'm glad I offered," she said.

"So am I."

"You miss her."

"Every minute of every day."

"Have you considered remarrying?"

He faced her. The hollowness beneath his cheekbones startled her. She knew then that the pain she'd seen in his eyes hadn't been her fanciful imagination.

Feeling somewhat at a disadvantage, she stood.

"Losing her fucking sucked," he said, palpable anguish making his voice raw. "No way will I take that chance again. Is that what you wanted to hear?"

"I'm sorry for your loss." She chose her words with care. "I can't imagine how bad it hurts."

He exhaled. "Thank you for that," he said. "A lot of well-meaning people have fed me platitudes."

Which, no doubt, was one of the reasons he spent time alone. "If you want to talk about her, please feel free."

"You're a persistent woman, Brandy."

"Most people use the word annoying," she said with a trace of a smile.

He responded in kind. "I was being polite."

She slid the soap into its dish and took down the showerhead. "May I?"

"I'm enjoying it," he said, facing away from her again.

She suspected they both needed the emotional reprieve. She took her time rinsing him, directing the warm water over his shoulders then moving the spray back and forth, going lower with each pass, making sure every bit of lather was gone. Then she asked him to turn around.

Brandy reached for the soap. She was glad he'd told her about Eleanor and about where he stood when it came to relationships, but in a way she was sorry it had ruined the mood.

He caught her hand and put it on his chest. "Stop lollygagging and get on with it, beautiful sub."

Responding in kind, she asked. "Lollygagging, Sir?"

"You're supposed to be bathing me."

She appreciated every moment of touching him, his hands and chest. A neat line of hair arrowed downwards in an oh-so sexy way, leading her to his semi-flaccid penis. She caressed his shaven balls and silky skin, crouching to stroke his perineum. With each touch, his erection grew. She savoured the connection, the way each of them had the power to make the other respond. "I could get you really clean if your legs were farther apart."

"You need a bigger shower," he said.

"This seems about right to me, Sir." She was at his feet and couldn't move away.

"Hard to argue with that."

She made certain she'd reached every bit of him, touching, arousing, before rinsing him. "Towels are on the shelves near the door."

He exited to give her more space, and she rinsed off quickly, anxious to be with him again. While she wasn't accustomed to having a man around, this seemed natural.

When she'd turned off the water and pulled back the shower curtain, he wrapped her in a towel and helped her over the tub's rim. A white towel hung loose around his hips, making his skin tone a bit darker by contrast. Every time she saw him, she was struck by his decadent masculinity. "You do a lot of little things to take care of me, Sir," she said. Which drove her to serve him more. "It's unusual."

"Is it? A good Dom takes care of his sub, sees to her needs and comfort. It's not all about telling someone what to do and getting your rocks off."

"I'm not your sub," she said.

He put his thumb beneath her chin and tipped back her head. "I see only one Dom and one sub here and now. That would make you mine."

Her breath hitched.

"It's my pleasure to do certain things for you, sub. Allow me."

The rough edge to his statement told her it wasn't a request. "Thank you, Sir."

He dried her then plucked the clips from her hair and dropped them on the vanity top. "How sore is your cunt?"

Before she answered, he continued, "I can use your ass if you're too tender."

The idea of having him use her so thoroughly appealed on a primitive level. "I can do whatever you want, Sir, it's up—"

An unholy scream rent the air.

Chapter Five

Niles shoved her behind him and grabbed the doorknob. "What in the hell...?"

"It's okay, Sir," she said, putting a calming hand on his back. "Thanks for wanting to protect me, but that's just my other four-footed friend."

Heart thundering, telling himself there was no imminent danger, he turned to face her. "What the fuck is it, a mountain lion?"

"It's an ordinary household cat."

His pulse slowed to normal. "That noise came from a cat?"

"I warned you that I had more animals, but I should have been more specific. His name's Whisper."

"You've got a messed up sense of humour, Ms Hess."

"He doesn't like people much, so he stays outside when I have company. He comes in through the pet door when he's ready."

"And lets the entire neighbourhood know when he's back."

Brandy picked up the towel she'd somehow dropped when he'd pushed her back. She held the material near her chest. It didn't hide her breasts with their beaded nipples. Even though the material covered her pelvis, the fact he couldn't see her pussy intrigued him more. "Do we need to do anything with the cat?"

"As in?"

"Feed it? Put it outside and bar the entrance?"

"If you have any hope of sleeping, Whisper needs to come in. He'll claw the door or hang from the window screen."

"The one in your bedroom?"

"Yeah. He's pretty vocal."

"Does it measure on the earthquake scale?"

"Not much. I think last time it was only a two-point-three or something."

He grinned at her. He'd been involved with a fair number of women over the years—before Eleanor. And he had sisters. None of them had collected strays like Brandy did. The woman had a soft heart.

"I didn't ask," she said, her eyes going wide. "Crap. Are you allergic?"

"No."

"Do you hate cats? A lot of men do."

"That's not a moral judgement, right?"

"Answer the question, Sir."

She'd drawn her eyebrows together, and her anxiety radiated across the distance, almost as disturbing as the animal's shrieks.

"I'm okay with them. But the only pussy I want on my face when I wake up in the morning is yours."

"Oh, Sir."

Bracing her free hand on one of his shoulders, she eased herself up and leaned into him to kiss his cheek.

Shit. Coming here tonight had been a mistake. Staying was an even bigger one. Thinking beyond that bordered on stupidity. But here he was doing just that. The more time he spent with her, the more he wanted.

"I'll go feed Whisper," she said.

"You can leave that towel here."

She dropped it, baring herself to him.

Another mistake. He wanted to bend her over the vanity and fuck her with the energy churning in him.

The cat cried again. He shuddered. "Jesus. That sound could be a real mood killer," he said.

She glanced purposefully at his cock.

It was still hard and insistent. "To clarify, nothing will kill *my* mood when it comes to you." Not with her full, inviting curves. She'd confessed to having masturbated while thinking about him. He had done the same, thinking about her.

Niles spent a lot of time with models and actresses. Many sent signals, subtle as well as overt, that they were available for a hook-up. Truthfully, while those women were beautiful and performed well for his cameras, none of them appealed to him in the way Brandy did. There was a realness about her. No pretences. He hadn't had this kind of reaction to a woman since Eleanor.

Another screech grated on his spinal cord. "Go."

"You sure you still want to stay the night?"

"Try getting rid of me."

"I was hoping you'd say that." She touched the spot on his cheek where she'd kissed him.

He opened the door and the cat blazed through the opening. It wound around her ankles in a silver ribbon.

Then, seeming to realise she had company, the cat sat and stared at him. If he believed in personification, he'd say the feline glared. It tipped its head and looked at him with unblinking yellow eyes. "He's strange looking." One ear flopped over. The one that stood was missing a jagged chunk. "Let me guess, he found you and not the other way around."

"About a year ago he followed MW through the doggy door and he hasn't left since."

"So your strays are now adopting strays, is that how it works?"

"I hadn't thought of it that way."

"Maybe I should feed him," he said. "Make friends with him."

"Are you sure, Sir?"

"Where's the food?"

"In a container under the sink. Right-hand side, about half way back. You'll find a set of three food bowls near the refrigerator. His is the smallest. I only put in half a scoop since MW will eat whatever Whisper leaves. He's good at defending what he wants, but after he flicks his tail and walks away, his food becomes fair game."

"This is getting complicated, Brandy."

She looked at him. Her eyes were wide, luminous, intriguing. She worried her lower lip. "Yes, Sir. It is."

Because of her hesitation in answering, he knew that she understood the subtext. He was talking about so much more than her pets. "Do you have restraints?"

"I do, Sir."

"Get them out and put them on the nightstand."

She nodded.

He paused at the door and looked over his shoulder. "Braid your hair."

"Oh, yes, Sir."

The cat followed him from the room.

He found the nuggets right where she'd said. Whisper sat on his haunches near his bowl. He thumped his tail as he waited, as if telling Niles to hurry up.

As he took care of the cat, Niles was aware of the sounds she made. No doubt she was following his orders. There was an undeniable intimacy about sharing a bathroom and a bed. People kept secrets for a reason, and it was more difficult to keep them hidden when you occupied the same space.

Earlier this evening, he'd treated her hesitation with lightness, but he'd been aware of the riptide beneath the surface. Neither of them could pretend their encounter meant nothing.

She'd been clear that she hadn't had a man in her private space in the two years that she'd lived here. That meant she'd been hurt before and was intent on protecting herself. Had she moved from Denver, or had she run?

He was beginning to understand Damien's warning. But rather than being scared away, Niles wanted to know why she took care of pets instead of a family.

When he joined her in the bedroom, Brandy was on her knees. Her hair hung down her back in a long silky strand, and the restraints he'd requested were laid out.

Over the last few minutes, he hadn't lost much of his erection, but arousal returned at the sight of her nudity. She was looking at the floor, with her knees spread and the backs of her hands resting on her thighs. "Well done."

"Thank you, Sir."

Not that he'd expected anything different.

He closed the door and advanced towards her. "You're well trained."

"Thank you, Sir. I read a lot and watched a lot of videos. My refinement came from Gregorio."

Resentment slashed through him, shocking him with its intensity.

"We are good friends, Sir. He helped me through some rough times in the past, but there's never been anything between us."

"Keep it that way."

"Sir?" She looked up.

What the hell was he thinking? She was a submissive at an exclusive club. He couldn't tell her how to behave or who she could sleep with. But that didn't stop him wanting to.

"I have no intention of fucking Gregorio, Sir."

Time and again he was struck by how in tune she was with his thoughts and how quickly she responded with reassurances. He reached for her braid and drew her up by it. "I was out of line."

"There's no need to explain, Sir. I understand."

"Bend over the bed," he said.

As she moved into position, he picked up the pair of cuffs and walked to the far side of the mattress. "Give me your hands."

She extended her arms towards him, and he secured her in the soft restraints. "You may hold onto the bedding if needed."

"What are you going to do to me, Sir?" Her voice trembled with sweet huskiness of arousal.

"I'm going to fuck your tight ass."

She lifted her head. Desire made her pupils dilate, and her lips were parted. "Yes," she said.

"Lube?"

"In the bathroom linen closet."

"Remain where you are."

"I wouldn't have done otherwise, Sir."

He exited the room to find two dogs and a cat curled up outside the door, like sentries on duty. Dana lifted her head. Whisper blinked then ignored him. Damned MW lunged for his toes. "Don't you dare." His command was brusque and loud.

The Dachshund whined as if deprived of a favourite toy but lay back down.

Niles wondered if Brandy would feel compelled to come to his—or the dog's—rescue but she didn't move. "Good girl," he said to her after he'd returned to her. "I thought you might not follow my order."

"If you had wanted my help, you'd have let me know. But that doesn't mean I wasn't tempted, Sir."

He placed the lube and a couple of handtowels on the nightstand. "At the Den, you disobeyed one of my instructions."

Her hot body trembled.

"Do you remember what it was?"

"Yes, Sir. I came without permission."

"I promised you a punishment for it. Would you like to accept that now?"

"Yes, Sir, if it pleases you. I don't want it looming out there."

"I want you to remember this night for a long time."

"Master Niles, I will remember every moment with you." Since she was facedown, the mattress muffled her words, but it couldn't disguise the honesty or the pulse of need.

Response knifed through him, hot, quick, lethal.

He wanted this woman in a way he shouldn't. He'd hardened his soul. Men were fortunate to meet one incredible woman in their lifetime. But two? Impossible.

No matter how he told himself that, the words *what if* teased him.

With a brutal force that shocked him, he shoved them away. What he felt for Brandy was raw sexual energy. What red-blooded male wouldn't? She was naked, stretched over a bed, cuffed for him, hair waiting to be yanked. And her curves... Curves like hers would turn a saint into a sinner.

He reached for the detachment that he'd worn like a shroud since Eleanor's death. He'd scened with the hottest women on the planet in recent years, and he'd done so without entangling his emotions.

This was no different.

She shifted slightly, not enough that any Dom would scold her, more of a gentle movement to shift her weight and ensure his continued interest.

Niles took his belt from the jeans he'd discarded earlier. He laid the leather across her back. "It seems you're looking forward to this punishment."

She moaned a little. "Oh, yes," she said. "Sir, I am."

"How many stripes do you deserve, you greedy little sub?"

"Dozens, Sir."

"Dozens?"

"At least. How will I learn otherwise?"

He grinned. A woman with needs that matched his... That night at the Den, he'd forced her orgasm solely with the idea of beating her at a later date. Even as they'd scened, he'd been planning their next meeting. He'd had no idea he'd have the luxury of holding her in bed afterwards.

Niles slid his hand over her curved derrière.

"Mmm. Thank you, Sir."

He rubbed her skin, each pass becoming more vigorous.

"Sir is too kind."

"Selfish," he corrected. "I want to make sure your bottom isn't too sore for future spankings."

"You're turning me on, Sir."

No doubt. The tangy scent of her arousal reached him, making his cock even harder. It would take all his formidable concentration to get through her belting instead of fucking her.

He increased the friction until he was convinced she had plenty of circulation to minimise bruising.

"I love having your hands on me, Sir."

"You're an appreciative miss." He picked up the belt and folded it in half. He wanted to stand close to her and be exacting about the placement of each stroke.

He started slow, the first hit a whisper.

"Sir," she protested.

"Patience." He didn't blame her for wanting to get on with it.

Once he'd covered her buttocks and thighs, he increased the force and landed the next few in random places.

She took a deep breath.

"Will this teach you to hold back your orgasms?" he asked.

"I'm afraid not, Sir."

"No?"

"I'm incorrigible."

He grinned. Damn, he enjoyed this.

With greater force, he kissed her flesh with the supple leather. Her skin reddened, and she jerked. He caught her on the inner part of her right thigh.

She hissed then said, "Thank you."

Not wanting her to feel uneven, he adjusted his stance and smacked the inside of her left thigh.

He saw her toes curl against the hardwood. "Are you getting hot from this?"

"God, yes, Sir. Everything you do… You know my body."

Not as well as he intended to.

With his left hand, he stroked between her legs. Like a hussy, she moved backwards, using her body to silently ask for more. Her pussy was already wet. He slipped a finger inside her and pressed against her G-spot. "Didn't you get in trouble for wanton behaviour?" He pulled away.

"Sir! How is it my fault that you are irresistible?"

"I thought you were a well-trained sub."

"I thought so, too. Until you and your devilish ways showed up."

He stepped back, shook out the belt then swung it in a wide arc, letting it crack beneath her buttocks.

"Yum," she said. "You know what I want."

At this point, she wasn't the only one in danger of coming. The sight of her reddened skin, the sound of husky approval in her voice and the sharp scent of musk had him on the edge. If he took his dick in hand, he'd ejaculate on her heated buttocks. Not that the idea was without merit, but he wanted to fill her ass and possess her.

He continued the beating, increasing the ferocity. His hits weren't as brutal as they would be if he were truly punishing her.

"Oh, Sir…" She turned her head to one side. "You could do this to me all night."

"No doubt we'd both enjoy that. Six more. Count them out." When she'd said dozens, he hadn't planned to deliver that many. But he had, because he wanted to please her.

He blazed one across both buttocks.

"One, Sir." She sighed.

Then he hit the backs of her calves.

Her knees buckled. *"Fuck, Sir. Two."*

"More?"

"Four more to go, Sir. Give them to me."

"That's my girl."

She straightened her body position. He seared her with another stripe.

"Three incredible smacks, Sir."

He grinned. He'd given a lot of beatings in his life, and he'd never had a sub behave as she was. Some took it in silence unless he required they count aloud. Others screamed. Some whimpered and cried. But she encouraged, pleaded and let him know how much she appreciated his efforts.

He delivered the last three in quick succession, and she exhaled softly.

"Thank you." She craned her head to look at him. "You are going to do me. Right, Sir?" Her eyes were wide, luminous with her plea.

"Are you kidding me? My cock is rock hard." He tossed the belt to one side and donned a condom before squirting lube onto one palm. "Are you ready for me?"

"I have to have you, Sir."

"Then let me in." He lubricated a finger and eased past her sphincter muscle.

She moaned. "Nice," she said. "It's been too long since I've felt that."

"I should put a plug in you all the time."

"I'd be a turned-on mess, Sir, unable to think at all."

"You would be thinking," he contradicted. "About me pulling it out and stuffing my dick in you. You'd be obsessed by thoughts of my domination, wondering when it would happen, hoping you could survive that long."

She moaned. Her words were muffled when she said, "As always, you're right, Sir."

He eased out then re-entered her with two fingers, stretching her out.

"I'm desperate to come, Sir."

"I know." It was obvious. Her body was slack, supple. "But I want you to wait."

She turned her face downward and burrowed into the mattress.

"You can wait a little longer," he said. "Otherwise I'll withhold beatings and put you in a corner."

"A fate worse than death, Sir."

"Then control yourself."

"Then stop what you're doing to me, Sir," she retorted. "That's my only hope."

Even now, she was moving around, trying to rub her clit on the bedding. Christ, he liked how responsive she was. Perhaps every Dom turned her on, but he hoped not.

"I'm crazy for your touch," she said, as if she'd read his thoughts.

A fine sheen of perspiration dotted her spine. As he played with her, she writhed.

"Sir, you're putting me in a bad position."

"How's that?"

"I want to obey you, and I'm having more and more trouble."

"That is a conundrum," he said with no sympathy. He continued to finger-fuck her tight little hole. Truthfully, she wasn't the only one who couldn't last much longer. His balls were drawn up, and he was clenching his jaw to think about anything other than ramming into her. "Are you ready for me, gorgeous sub?"

"Sir, I've been ready. I could have taken you even without your generous preparation."

He lubed up his dick with a few strokes that had him gritting his teeth then wiped his hands on a nearby towel. Then he released her hands before instructing, "Reach back and part your buttocks."

She did, and he stood there for a few seconds, admiring the view, made even more compelling by the welts on her skin. "On your toes," he said. "Toes pointed in."

Brandy moved into position, exposing more of her pussy and puckered anal whorl. "I could come from looking at you," he said, his voice gruffer than normal.

"If that pleases you, Sir."

"Well said." He positioned his cockhead at her opening. "Spread wider."

Instantly she did.

He pushed in a few inches then moved back to give her a momentary break.

"Yum, Sir." She adjusted a bit to give him greater access.

"Beautiful." This time, he went in a little deeper.

She turned her head to the side.

"Stay in position," he said, though the command wasn't needed. She behaved with perfect grace.

He stroked in and out, inserting a bit more with each thrust, letting her accommodate him.

After several seconds, his control began to unravel. He wanted to fill her. All night, her proximity had caused long-dormant need to reignite. He hadn't wanted sex for more than a year after losing Eleanor. After that, masturbation had suited him fine. He'd had meaningless fucks since then, which took care of hormonal demands, but this raw desire for Brandy was new.

"I want to feel your balls against me."

He grabbed her buttocks and parted her even farther.

"Give it to me, Sir."

Surging forward, he did, burying himself to the hilt.

"Ahh," she said, the single word a purr of approval.

He remained still for a moment until she said, "More."

"Hands above your head," he told her.

She struggled for a moment but did as he'd ordered.

He wound the length of her hair around one of his hands.

"You're so masterful, Sir."

She clutched at the bedding as he pulled on her hair and rocked his pelvis. "Can you come from anal penetration?" he asked her.

"I never have. But I do love it."

"You doing okay?"

"Want…"

With his free hand, he grabbed one of her shoulders. With him filling her rear, holding her hair, she was his.

He leant forward and sank his teeth into the side of her neck.

"Fuck!" she screamed.

She bucked beneath him, forcing her butt up. She parted her legs more, bringing her body lower so that she was more open to him and her clit was pressed against the bed. Her uninhibited motions urged him on. This woman loved sex and was ultra-honest about what she wanted and needed. He respected that.

He bent his knees for more leverage then surged up inside her.

"Oh yes. Sir, Sir, if I can come—"

"If you can, do." He moved in her with short motions, just enough to get sufficient distance to surge and bury himself balls deep.

"That's what I wanted," she said, the words strangled in gasps.

She pushed back, in concert with him, helping him to get and stay deeper.

"Damn, damn, *damn.*"

"Too much?"

"No. Overwhelmed. Good."

Her legs trembled and she bent her knees, pressing herself more into the mattress. He released her shoulder and forced his hand beneath her pelvis to push against her swollen clit.

She jerked then her body froze. "I..."

"Come," he commanded, yanking on her hair, briefly abrading her clit then surging up inside her.

Brandy screamed and her body stiffened.

Her internal muscles constricted him in the best possible way.

"That's my sub," he said, still holding onto her but with less pressure. He leaned over so he was close to her ear. "First anal orgasm."

"I'd say thank you, but I don't even remember my own name right now."

He kissed her ear. "Well done. And your name's Brandy."

She gulped in a breath. "I want to satisfy you, Sir."

"The way you came just about emasculated me."

"I'm not going to apologise," she said.

"Hell and back, you'd better not. That was hot, Ms Hess."

"I think I'll sleep for a week."

"I'll hold you while you do."

"Come in me, Sir." She ground against him as an added invitation.

He was helpless to resist her. Niles captured her hips and kept her steady as he surged inside her ass.

"I had no idea," she said.

Once he had her where he wanted her, he once again twisted his hand in her luxurious hair.

He brought his other hand around and put his forearm beneath her chest to lift her torso from the mattress.

Without him needing to tell her what to do, she leant back to rest her head on his chest. She reached around to put a palm against his neck and curled her other hand into his biceps.

They were linked on physical level, and more.

"Oh...so, so deep," she told him. "It's..."

She didn't seem to have words. Nor did he. He was a man possessed by a savage urge that only this woman could sate.

"Yes, yes," she said.

Holding her tight, he thrust into her ass. "You respond so well to me, Brandy."

"Because you're unbelievably demanding, Sir."

His cock thickened as his blood heated. It seemed incredible that she could feel him so completely.

Sweat beaded on his brow and all his muscles strained from the force. Brandy in his arms, he buried himself to his testicles and squeezed his eyes shut as ejaculate spurted in pulse after relentless pulse.

He felt her body tremble beneath his as she struggled to keep her feet on the ground and not collapse against him. For long seconds, he held her even though common sense encouraged him to let her go. He prided himself on never losing control. But the connection with Brandy unravelled him. It was more than her sexy body, greater than her compassion. It was her quirkiness, the way she trusted him and made him look inside himself. "You okay?" he asked.

"Never better, Sir." She arched back into him.

"I might have been too rough."

"Not at all, Sir. If I had needed to, I would have used a safe word."

He withdrew his spent cock and lowered her to the mattress. She made an odd sound as she curled into a ball. "Was that a purr?"

"It was."

"I'll be right back." He was grinning.

"I guarantee you, I'm not going anywhere, Sir."

Outside the door, Dana looked at him and whimpered. "Promise I didn't hurt her," he told the dog. MW leapt up and dived for Niles' toes. He snapped his fingers and pointed at the floor. The dog yipped a couple of times, but settled down. The cat thumped its tail once but didn't crack an eyelid.

Niles had never had an army of four-footed protectors looking after one of his subs. He wasn't sure what to make of it, but he didn't mind. That surprised him.

He turned on the faucet and disposed of the condom. After he'd cleaned up, he reached for a washcloth and ran it under the water then grabbed a small towel on the way out.

All of the pets had inched closer to the bedroom, and he debated what to do. He'd never had animals growing up. While he and Eleanor had talked about getting a puppy, the time had never been right.

In the end, he left the door open a crack. Brandy was still in the same position, and the sight of her reddened, well-used body stirred an unfamiliar instinct to protect. "I don't want to startle you," he said as he sat on the bed.

"I'm awake," she said.

"Uh-huh." He pressed a heated washcloth to her.

She yelped. "That's hot."

"Warm," he countered. "You'll be grateful in the morning." He kept the cloth in place until it cooled then dried her with the fresh towel.

"I should have done that for you," she protested.

"With your super-power energy?"

"Yeah. That." With a yawn, she rolled to face him. "Thank you, Sir."

"Rest," he told her, trailing his thumb over one of her eyebrows.

"The towels go in the laundry basket in the closet. And close the door."

"Pets?"

"They'll steal everything including my shoes, and I have a couple of fabulous pairs you haven't seen yet."

"The thought of you in a pair of shoes and nothing else is enough to keep me awake all night," he said as he found the laundry basket, then joined her on the bed. "Do you sleep with your hair in a braid?"

"Most times, yes. It saves me time in the morning. If you prefer it loose, I don't mind at all."

"You sure?"

"Positive."

"Face away from me."

She did. He pulled off the band and pulled each of the three strands loose. Then he spread his fingers and used them as a comb. He'd never played with a woman's hair before, other than to hold it during sex or smooth it while giving a hug. Reluctant to let her go, he massaged her head.

"I'll give you all night to finish doing that, Sir."

He continued for a few moments, enjoying the quiet and her gentle sounds. Niles hadn't realised how much he'd missed having a woman in his bed.

Her breathing evened out, and he knew she'd fallen asleep.

Brandy, he quickly learnt, wasn't easy to disturb. He pulled up a blanket and tucked it around her without her seeming to be aware. After turning off the light, he tugged her against him.

* * * *

When dawn brightened the sky the next morning, she was still cocooned next to his body. For a few minutes, he stayed where he was, enjoying the peace, the quiet solitude of the mountain morning and having a sexy sub snuggled next to him, with her blonde hair spilling across the dark blue pillow in an inviting contrast. He considered fisting her hair and pulling back her head and kissing her long and deep. That would be a hell of a way to start a Sunday. Not just this Sunday, any Sunday.

That thought startled him.

He was thinking beyond today. This was a first for him. In business, he was always doing projections and forecasts, but he'd shut off his personal life since Eleanor's funeral on that grey, snowy morning three years ago.

A dog's nails clicked against the hardwood floor.

Not wanting to disturb Brandy, Niles climbed out of bed, grabbed his jeans then headed down the hallway. Brandy didn't move.

In the kitchen, Dana stretched her long legs in front of her and yawned wide enough to swallow a small country.

Whisper was nowhere in sight.

MW dashed out of the doggie door.

Because he'd spent so much time in the kitchen last night, it didn't take long to locate the bag of coffee or the filters. Within a minute, strong brew was hissing and spitting into the carafe. He watched it as if that would hurry the maker along.

A seeming eternity later, he poured himself a cup before going outside.

Dana yawned and traipsed after him. MW dashed over to nip at his toes, and Niles commanded, "Sit."

The dog bared his teeth but sat.

He took a seat to watch the remnants of the sunrise and both dogs wandered around the yard. Dana cocked her head and looked at a deer. MW chased it off, nipping at its hooves. "You're a little terror, aren't you?"

Dana curled up at his feet. Once the mule-tailed deer was out of sight, MW returned. Niles wasn't certain a dog could look smug, but this one did.

A few minutes later, he heard the back door close. He turned to see Brandy, hair everywhere, a cup of coffee in hand. She'd dressed in a blue cowl neck T-shirt and black yoga pants, so tight and clingy she could have been poured into them. Her nipples were beaded. Like him, her feet were bare.

"Mind if I join you?" she asked. "Or would you prefer some alone time?"

"I've been offering the dogs treats if they'd be loud enough to wake you up."

She smiled.

He hooked his foot on a nearby chair and dragged it closer to him. Then when she went to sit, he changed his mind. He captured her body and pulled her onto his lap.

With a laugh, she moved her cup aside so that her drink sloshed on the ground rather than on either of them.

"Morning, sub."

"Fabulous good morning to you, Sir." She looped one arm around him and nuzzled his neck.

Her hair tickled his chest. And her body curled alluringly against his.

"Thank you for taking care of the dogs and for letting me sleep those few extra minutes…" She re-situated herself so she was more comfortable. "Oh, and for brewing coffee. You could be the perfect Dom."

"Anything for such a delectable sub."

"Can I make it up to you?"

Since his cock was already thickening he said, "I may have an idea or two."

"I was hoping you did."

He reached down and picked up his cooled cup of coffee.

"Shall I go sit over there?"

"Not a chance."

For a long time, neither of them said anything, content to watch the pets and the occasional wary deer.

"Go with me to a silent auction Friday night?"

"I beg your pardon, Sir?"

"I need a gorgeous date. Dinner, dancing. At the Moline downtown." Until the words came out of his mouth, he'd had no real intention of attending the event. His aunt, Mame, chaired the event every year. He and Eleanor had been regulars, but since her death, he'd begged off.

This year, his aunt had informed him she'd reached the end of her patience. If he didn't show up of his own free will, she would come to his house and drag him into her limo by his ear. He didn't underestimate the steamroller that was Mame. "You'd be doing me a huge favour." He smoothed Brandy's hair back from her face so he could see her expression.

"The Moline?" she repeated. The hotel was one of Denver's newest boutique hotels, fancy, upscale, with only a couple of dozen rooms, all costing four figures for a one-night stay. It was located on the Sixteenth Street Mall, so many of the rooms overlooked one of the most fun, hippest, freakiest areas of town. She loved the fact that, on any given night, it was possible to see a wide range of humanity, from homeless people and up-and-coming buskers, to sports stars, executives and politicians. Since there were some excellent restaurants along the street, almost anyone who stayed in downtown Denver could be seen passing by.

"I'm confused, Sir. Do you want me to attend as your submissive?"

"Good God, no. As my companion."

"I'm not sure what to say."

"Yes is the perfect answer."

She pursed her lips. "Maybe I don't know how to behave in public."

"Try again."

"Maybe you don't want me to get to know your friends. How will I answer questions about how we know each other, where we met, what I do for a living?"

With the mutinous set of her jaw and the way she worried a strand of hair, he read her anxiety. Coming from someone so self-assured, the reaction shocked him. "There will be no questions."

"It's not that easy, Sir."

"It is," he countered.

"Maybe for someone who lives life like you do," she countered.

He went still. She was walking a tightrope, between expressing her fears and pissing him off. Keeping his flash of frustration under control, he tightly asked, "What the hell does that mean?"

"Look, Sir, I didn't mean to offend you. We don't move in the same social circles. I love to scene with you, and I appreciate your coming to my barbecue, but a fundraiser at the Moline isn't my thing."

"Why not? Great food and expensive champagne, along with an excellent dancing companion."

Even that didn't elicit a smile from her.

"Most of it will be filled with boring and insipid conversation."

"Which is exactly why I need you to go with me."

"I don't do pretentious anymore, Sir. Not that I ever did it well." She slid from his lap and went to her own chair, putting some distance between them.

He chose his words with great care. "That sounds a bit defensive."

"Does it? Maybe it is."

Like she had earlier, she looped some strands of hair around a finger.

"I told you I moved up here about two years ago. It was after Reyes Northrup and I broke up."

He whistled. Reyes' father had made money—lots of it—in oil a long time ago. His trophy wife and kids lived high off the profits.

"His mother never pretended to like me."

"Shawndra is a social climber and a bitch," he said.

"You know her?"

"Well enough to know you can't take her personally."

"I don't." Brandy gave him a ghost of a smile. "She also cares about her kids."

He wondered how many times she'd repeated those words to herself. "So, she's a saint."

"No. But she has always done what she thought was best for her family. I can't fault her for that. Reyes is a sweet guy with a big heart."

"Who can't stand up to his mommy and has a hell of a drug problem."

"That's a bit harsh."

"It's the truth," he countered. He had a lot of respect for people who earned their way in life, but none at all for guys who lived off their trust funds.

"I thought I could save him. Tried to, time and again. But when everything is magnified under the spotlight of the tabloid press, it makes it that much harder. That last night..."

"The Great Disaster?"

"You remembered."

"I've told you. I remember everything about you."

Brandy stood and began to pace. MW jumped up and nipped at her toes.

"Sit," he told the pest.

The dog plopped down, though he continued to move his head, tracking her feet.

Patience wasn't Niles' normal forte, but for Brandy, he'd try.

"I arrived home from work around midnight and found Reyes unconscious in the shower. I called an ambulance, and I held his hand all the way to the hospital. His mother met us in the emergency room. She made it clear that she blamed me and my lifestyle for his problems."

"Lifestyle?"

"She didn't know I was a submissive or that Reyes liked to tie up women."

"So…"

"I was working at a sports bar to help pay for college."

"And the alcohol was a bad influence?"

"Waiting tables would have been scandalous enough, but it's the type of place where the women wear white button-down shirts and ridiculously short kilts."

"Do you still have it?"

"Pervert," she said.

"Red-blooded male," he corrected.

She gave him a wan smile and shook her head. But thankfully, the pain he'd witnessed on her face had been wiped away.

"He was there for a bachelor party. He was flirting with me. At the end of the night, his friends decided to go to Central City to play some craps, but he said he was too drunk to go with them. So I took him home— to my place. It wasn't until much later that I realised he'd been doing something stronger than shots. Sorry. Am I boring you?"

"Not at all."

"I can—"

"Go on," he told her in the no-nonsense tone that he reserved for business negotiations.

"The next day we went to pick up his car. He was apologetic, wanted to thank me and make it up to me, so he took me to dinner. Despite the differences in our backgrounds, I convinced myself that we could make it work, that my love would help him get better, see how much brighter life could be. Before long, we fell into a pattern. He'd get arrested or messed up, and I'd rescue him. He'd be remorseful and promise never to do it again."

"But he always did," Niles surmised.

She took a seat, perching on the edge. "He took me to a family dinner, and when his mom asked what I did for a living, I told her." She smiled. "It was like a scene from a movie. His younger sister knew of the place. His mother put down her fork and pushed away her plate. His dad raised his eyebrows and said he'd been there once or twice. She told me to my face that I wasn't good enough for her son. And she asked him why he insisted on dating a trollop. To make the story shorter, we didn't stay for dessert."

"That was the night of the overdose?"

"No. We continued to see each other after that, but we avoided his family, something else she blamed me for—taking away her son."

"She wasn't good at accepting reality," Niles observed.

"Anyway, in the emergency room, she called security and had me escorted out. She was next of kin." Brandy shrugged. "There was nothing I could do. I telephoned for updates, but she'd forbidden the nurses to answer my questions. When he called me the next day, he was, as always, sorry for what had happened, but said he was tired of fighting with his mother and he hoped I understood."

Even though she had the distance of years, he still saw confusion in her eyes.

"Last I heard through mutual friends, he's headed to rehab on the West Coast before he marries a hotel heiress."

"Not everyone is like the Northrups," he said.

"Of course not. You're not. Neither is Master Damien."

"If you'll go with me, I promise to stay by your side."

"That's not a factor for me. I can take care of myself, Sir. I've been doing it for a long time."

"And doing a great job of it. I know I'm being selfish by asking you to go with me, but with you there, I might enjoy the function. And…" He decided to use every tactic in his arsenal. "Since you like taking care of others, you can tell yourself you're doing a friend a favour. In fact, at the grocery store, you told me you'd owe me a favour if I manned the barbecue."

She scowled.

"Pay up," he countered. "Unless you want to earn a reputation as someone who reneges on her word?"

"That's unfair, Sir."

"I play to win. You already know that." He smiled in what he hoped was a charming way. "And I want you to go with me."

"Do any rules apply to you, Sir?"

"None."

She exhaled.

"At least think about it."

"Sir…"

"Please?"

Brandy closed her eyes. "You're relentless."

"When I want something, I get it."

"I haven't agreed to go with you."

"You will. I'll even buy you breakfast as a way to sweeten the deal."

"What?"

"John told me his pecan waffles have been rated amongst the top in the state."

"It's probably not what you're expecting. It's more of a diner than a restaurant. I can make us some eggs here."

"Are you calling me a snob again, Brandy? You might want to watch your words. You're starting to annoy me."

"I—"

"Do you have fishnet stockings?"

"I do. But if I wear them, my legs will get cold."

At least she was no longer arguing about going out to eat. "Did I ask if you'd be comfortable?"

She shifted then lowered her eyes. "No, Sir."

"You've got five minutes to get ready to go." When she didn't immediately move, he said, "That's it. Get your clothes off and lie across my lap."

"What?"

He levelled his gaze on her. "Do I need to repeat myself?"

Slowly she stood.

She stripped off her top and dropped it on the chair behind her.

"Bra," he said. Breath constricted in his throat. This woman. He wondered what the hell was wrong with him. The more he had her, the more he wanted. This kind of attraction had never happened for him before. He felt as if he'd combust if he didn't touch her, taste her, possess her.

She unclasped the lingerie and shrugged from it. The cool air puckered her nipples. He was mesmerised. "I think we should have a bonfire where we burn all your brassieres."

"If you say so, Sir."

A sensual undertone made her voice husky and it laced straight through him.

She removed the yoga pants with the finesse of an exotic dancer.

"Torture," he said.

It took an agonising amount of time for her to finish undressing.

"Let me look at you," he said.

Goosebumps had formed on her flesh. Despite that, she widened her stance and placed her hands behind her neck then arched her back to thrust out her breasts.

"You're sensational," he told her. He made a circle with his forefinger, and she complied with the unspoken order, turning her back towards him.

Perfectly reading his mind, she grabbed her ankles. Her rear bore no traces of their night together. "Come to me."

She rose then pivoted before sauntering towards him in a purposeful and provocative way.

Instead of casting her gaze down, she met his eyes.

"Do you have any idea how much power you hold over me?" As he asked the question, he realised even he had no idea.

Brandy draped herself across his lap and adjusted herself, each time tilting up her ass higher and higher. No doubt she was hoping to drive him crazy. It was working.

"Enough," he snapped, the word sounding like a growl.

Dana made an odd sound and tilted her head. MW dashed over to see what was going on. Even Whisper slinked onto the patio from beneath a bush.

"Go away," she told the animals.

None of them obeyed her.

"Now," he snapped.

They all moved back.

"You're going to have to share your tricks with me," she said.

"Just glad it works on you as well as them," he replied.

He rubbed her butt cheeks until she made sounds of pleasure.

"Oh, Sir."

Mindful of the chill in the air, he brought his hand down across her ass half a dozen times in quick succession. She remained in place, and her sounds became soft whimpers. She adjusted herself in order to rub against his thigh. "Getting turned on?"

"Yes." The word was forced out past a gasp.

He liked having her here, in his arms, their bodies intimately connected through trust. After another few spanks to remind them both of the natural order of things, he helped her to sit up.

She curled into him, her glorious hair spilling across his chest. He held her tight and rubbed her arms and legs.

"You can get almost anything from me when you do that," she said. She tilted her head to look back at him.

She smiled in a way so enchanting he'd happily wrap up the universe for her.

"Especially if you were to give me an orgasm, Sir."

"No chance. I want you aroused through breakfast."

"I will be," she assured him.

Which meant she would go with him. He brushed hair back from her face so he could look at her expression.

"You know how to touch me, Sir."

"If I had my choice, Brandy, I'd never stop." Still holding her, he stood and walked towards the house.

"Put me down, Sir! You can't carry me all the way inside."

"Actually, I believe I can."

The dogs leapt up and barked as they trailed behind. The cat twitched its ragged ear and flicked its tail in disinterest.

Brandy giggled as she reached for the doorknob and pushed open the back door. "In the movies, it's not quite this complicated," she said.

Once the dogs were inside, he kicked the door closed and continued through the house to the bedroom where he deposited her on the edge of the mattress.

"About those fishnet stockings…"

Chapter Six

"Stay there," Master Niles said as he parked the sports utility vehicle near Margot and John's restaurant.

Brandy had been reaching for the door handle but dropped her hand. If he wanted to treat her like royalty, who was she to complain?

She watched him walk around the hood, the sun making streaks of gold appear in his dark brown hair. The heated leather seats were a luxury she could get accustomed to in no time. She'd worn the stockings he'd wanted, and she wasn't at all chilled.

He opened her door and offered his hand as she exited. She slid her palm against his, feeling his strength. Damn. The man was so sexy and thoughtful.

"Maybe we should have had sex before we left," he said against her ear, his voice gruff. "I'm not sure how I'll get through the meal."

A sensual thrill uncurled in her pussy. He made her feel vibrant and sexy.

He kept his fingers against the small of her back as they entered the diner. From the cash register area, Margot waved, her eyes wide.

"Have a seat anywhere," she said.

Not that there were many choices. Even though it was early, the place was almost packed.

They selected the last table near a window, and he held her chair while she was seated.

A harried-looking waitress came over, a coffee carafe already in hand. "Something to drink besides coffee? Orange juice?"

"Coffee would be great," Brandy said. "I didn't have enough before I was hurried out the door."

Master Niles turned over the mugs that were already on the table. The waitress filled both.

"I'll be back for your orders."

He took a sip but didn't look at the menu. Instead, he regarded her with his usual intensity. Despite her best efforts, she squirmed. Everything about him made her hyperaware of being female and submissive.

It stunned her how well he fitted in with her life. She'd been crazy in love with Reyes, and they'd lived together for a time in his exclusive Cherry Creek town home. She'd never felt comfortable there. It had been as if she were a little girl playing house. In retrospect, Reyes hadn't done anything to make her feel more secure. When she'd pointed out the differences in their lifestyles, he'd told her to get over herself. And when his mother had stopped by unexpectedly one day, finding Brandy on her knees and all but naked, she'd said it was a good thing Brandy knew her place.

Reyes had laughed off Brandy's indignity and excused his mother's attitude. That had been much better than answering questions about his BDSM proclivities.

Unlike Master Niles, Reyes had expected her to fit into his life, but he'd never returned the favour. He hadn't wanted to go fishing with her dad or hang out with her friends. When they'd been invited to parties, she'd had to go alone.

Master Niles, though he lived in those same social circles, couldn't be more different.

Inviting him to her gathering had been an impulse. She'd hoped that they would have wild, kinky sex afterwards, but she'd never expected he'd spend the night or that he'd want to continue to hang out.

Earlier, while she'd done her hair and dressed, he'd fed the dogs then gone back outside to collect their forgotten cups and her discarded clothing.

When she'd exited the bedroom, she'd found that he'd already started the car and turned on the heater so she didn't get cold.

If she wasn't careful, she might start to fall for this man. He satisfied her sexually and she loved his relentless dominance, along with his old-world manners.

As of this morning, she'd yet to see the ghosts of his past in his eyes. Dare she hope that she was as good for him as he was for her?

"Hey," Margot said, joining them with a cup of coffee in hand.

Master Niles stood until after she'd taken her seat.

"Hope you're not trying to impress me," Margot said. "I know who you really are."

"A world-class asshole?" he guessed, resuming his seat.

"Jesus, Margot. Don't make me sorry we came here."

"No," Margot said, ignoring Brandy. "That was Reyes. Since you stepped foot through our door, you're a second-string asshole at best."

Brandy blushed furiously. "We can leave, Sir," she told him.

"You're seriously calling him Sir?"

"Enough," Brandy said.

"Relax, sub. Margot can bare her teeth all she wants. She doesn't scare me."

"I should. I can be the biggest bitch on the planet."

Brandy collapsed against the seatback. Coming here with Niles might count as one of the biggest mistakes she'd ever made.

"I like how protective you are," he said.

Margot grinned. "Yeah. But this doesn't mean I like you," she added.

"Never assumed it did."

"Or what you do."

"So you've watched some of my videos with your husband?" he replied.

Brandy grabbed her porcelain mug as if it were a lifeline.

"I'd be happy to provide you both with some instruction. Or maybe Brandy could."

"Dying here," Brandy said with a laugh. Master Niles could hold his own.

"I don't trust you," Margot continued.

"You don't have to," Master Niles said easily. "The only opinion that counts is Brandy's."

"Well said," Brandy agreed. She looked at her friend and jerked her head towards the cash register. "Don't you have work to do?"

"Yeah, yeah."

"And why don't you make yourself useful and take our order?"

Before Margot could respond, Niles said, "I'll try your award-winning pecan waffles. With bacon and two eggs, poached."

Margot nodded.

"Eggs Benedict," Brandy said. After Margot left the table, Brandy continued, "You had to know you were in for this."

"Yes, I did."

"So why did you insist we come?"

"For you."

"For me?"

"John and Margot matter to you. It doesn't matter what John told her last night, she had to challenge me and let me know that you're loved and cared for. I respect that."

He'd done it for her?

Their waitress splashed fresh coffee into their cups and moved on to the next table without pausing.

"Is this part of your bribe?" she asked, narrowing her eyes.

"Is it working?"

"You're impossible, Sir."

He took a drink of his coffee.

The diner grew noisier as more people showed up. After a while, there was a wait for a table, which was good because Margot was occupied at the cash register. Even John was too busy to leave the kitchen and say hello.

A moose wandered by in the distance, and patrons crowded against the windows to watch it. Dozens of cell phones were whipped out for pictures. Since one young couple was nearby, Master Niles asked them to take a photo of them.

They leaned close, touching their heads together. The woman said, "Smile!" before snapping the picture and returning his phone.

He looked at the snapshot then showed it to her. She'd seen worse. At least her eyes were open.

"Using it as my background," he said, swiping his finger across the glass surface.

The man surprised her all the time.

Even though the place was hopping, breakfast was hot and perfectly prepared.

"John was right to brag about the waffles," Master Niles said, pouring on more maple syrup and slathering the surface with butter. "Bite?"

"There's already plenty of calories in this meal," she protested. "I'll need a ton of exercise if I eat anything more," she said.

"That can be arranged."

He stabbed a piece with his fork and offered it across the table to her. She closed her mouth around the sweetness.

"I love to watch you enjoy yourself."

She couldn't imagine Reyes ever having behaved this way.

"Let's go work off breakfast." He picked up the bill the waitress had dropped off.

At the cash register, Margot said, "You might not be all bad. But I'm not ready to give you my stamp of approval."

He handed over his credit card. "Fair enough."

* * * *

At home, he took her to the bedroom.

"I like the stockings. I was looking at your legs every chance I got. Thank you for wearing them."

"I would do anything you said, Sir."

"Then leave them on while we have sex."

"Of course." She undressed, aware of his approving gaze. Then she stood in front of him, in only the stockings and a garter belt.

"I've never needed a woman this bad," he said.

"May I help you undress?"

After a moment, in which she wondered if he'd refuse, he nodded.

She tugged his shirt over his head and hung it from a bedpost. Then she unbuckled his belt, remembering the feel of that worn leather on her bare skin. She'd happily submit to that any day.

He toed off shoes then removed his socks before she released the button at his waistband. His dick was already getting harder and she wanted to reach inside his jeans and touch him. "So, so tempting…"

"No," he said.

Which only made her want him more, and he had to know it. Within seconds, she had him nude.

"How sore are you?" he asked when he'd donned a condom.

She sat on the edge of the bed, naked, waiting, willing.

"Tell the truth. I'll know otherwise."

"Don't you miss anything?"

"Not when it comes to you."

He was so delicious, she wanted him everywhere. She didn't know when or if she'd see him again and she wanted to enjoy each moment. Still, he folded his arms across his chest, and she knew better than to lie to him. "My ass is tender."

"And your cunt?"

"Fine, Sir. Honest."

"On all fours. I want to play with your tits while I fuck you."

Her insides liquefied. The way he looked at her and the authority in his tone were a lethal combination.

The bedsprings groaned as he climbed on the bed behind her. She turned her head to look at him, even though she knew she shouldn't. "You look hot, Sir," she said. He held his thick cock in one hand. The sight of his powerful thighs and broad chest made her hungry. "Please, Sir," she said.

Then his cockhead was against her opening.

He placed a hand on her hip to hold her steady. As he eased into her he grabbed a handful of her hair, his fingers on her scalp.

This position felt primitive. It had never been her favourite before, but it was now.

"Keep still."

"Sorry, Sir." She hadn't realised she'd arched her back, begging for his penetration.

He began to rock them, and he went in deeper and deeper each second.

The fact he'd imprisoned her made the sensations all the more overwhelming.

Finally he was all the way in. He kept her in place for a full thirty seconds. A gamut of emotions tumbled through her — impatience, desire, confusion. Finally she transcended the turmoil and submitted, body and soul. If he wanted to keep her here forever, she'd do it without question.

She became aware of the width of his cock pulsing inside her, the strength of his grip and the rhythm of his breath.

By the time he began to move, her whole body was aware of him.

He started with short strokes, and by the time he lengthened them enough to pull out and thrust all the way back in, her pussy was drenched. "Oh, Sir."

"You're a gorgeous sub." He released his grip on her hip. "Remain as you are."

She liked it better when he held her. It made it easier for her to let go mentally and physically. This required her active participation.

He plumped her left breast then squeezed her nipple. She wanted to shove her hips backwards.

"Don't move," he reminded her.

Brandy wasn't sure what the hell he was doing to her...besides driving her mad. "I'm not sure how much longer I can last, Sir."

He reacted with lightning speed. Within moments, he was on his back, and she was straddling him with his penis inside her. She felt disoriented.

"Put your hands behind your back."

Once she had, he pinched her nipples and rotated them. She hissed a breath between her clenched teeth.

"Come all you want. Fuck me."

Most Doms didn't allow her to do this. She savoured the headiness, using her toes and knees for balance as she rose and descended in a way that put pressure on her G-spot.

"Fuck me," he encouraged.

She watched his face, and when he closed his eyes, she rode him hard. "You fill me up. So, so deep, Sir." At some point, she thought he might take over, hold her waist or at least tell her what to do, but he didn't. He let her have control.

With great gusto, she did as he'd said, rising, slamming herself down.

"You don't need permission."

She leant forward, and he moved to grip her shoulders, supporting her. She came with a shattered scream.

"That's it, my gorgeous sub."

He let her stay where she was and she gulped for air. She had no idea how long she stayed like that, but his eyebrows were drawn together and her weight was braced on her elbows. "What day is it?" she asked.

Master Niles chuckled. "Guess it was good for you."

"Now I want it to be good for you." She dug her knees in next to his hips and used that for leverage to straighten up.

He needed no further encouragement to take over. Grabbing her waist, he lifted her up then pulled her down on his throbbing cock.

They rocked the bed and each other.

She was panting.

He tightened his jaw. "Love your cunt," he said, words nearly indistinguishable from each other.

The momentum made another orgasm build inside her.

"Yeah. Squeeze my dick with your hot pussy."

Her hair fell everywhere in a tangled mess. He surged a final time, forcing her down and keeping her there.

With a guttural moan, he spurted.

"Fuck," he said later, after he'd relaxed his muscles. He wrapped his arms around her and pulled her down on his sweat-slickened body.

Then he cradled her head between his hands and kissed her, gently teasing her tongue.

"That was like a cherry on top of an ice cream sundae. That kiss," she explained when he rose one eyebrow. "You know, when you think it can't get any better, it becomes even more incredible."

She pushed her hair behind her ears and slowly climbed off him then left the bed with great reluctance.

As she shrugged into a robe, he said, "Count your blessings any time I let you wear any clothes. Wait. Don't fasten the belt."

She dropped her hands to her sides.

He stood and discarded the condom then traced a finger across the top of one of her stockings. "This is the view I'll carry with me until I see you again."

Her heart shoved six beats into the space of a second. All day she'd pretended they wouldn't say goodbye, and the truth was, she didn't know if she'd see him again. She wanted to, hoped to, but wasn't sure it was possible outside of the Den.

Since he lived in Denver, running into each other at the grocery store had been a one-off chance. She wasn't inclined to give up her pets or home, and his business interests kept him in Denver. Even without that, she had no intention of fitting into his life with its social demands.

"I will see you again," he assured her, as if he'd read her mind.

"Yes, Sir." She blinked, severing the connection. Her motions mechanical, she dressed and walked him to the door. The dogs followed, and Master Niles took the time to pet both of them before climbing into his SUV.

She waved from the carport. He crooked his finger, and she hurried over to him.

"I mean it," he said.

He held her jaw in one hand and brought her in for a kiss.

As he drove away, Dana lay down and put her big head on her outstretched paws. MW bit Brandy's bare toes.

She found a couple of toys and threw them as far as she could. Neither dog chased them. "Fine lot we are," she told the animals.

* * * *

Night didn't come soon enough, and she took a long bubble bath to pass the time. Not that it helped. She'd drained the water heater, and the book she'd carried in there couldn't keep her attention.

In a ridiculously short amount of time, he'd insinuated himself into her life, a fact even more apparent the next morning when she had to brew the coffee. She'd liked having a pot sitting on the burner waiting for her.

She took her cup outside to watch the sunrise and tried to put the weekend behind her. That wasn't as easy as she'd hoped when Margot telephoned.

"So, has that guy called you yet?" Margot demanded.

"You mean Master Niles?"

"Yeah, yeah. Niles."

"Don't you have a restaurant to open?"

"It's Monday. We're closed. So. I didn't hate him as much as I thought I would."

"That's high praise coming from you."

"But now I think he's an asswipe since he hasn't called you."

"I didn't say that," Brandy protested.

"You didn't have to. Let me know if you want to have lunch or a drink. I'd suggest a hike but my feet hurt like hell from the new heels I wore yesterday."

"I'm good."

"If you fucking mope like you did after Reyes, I'm kidnapping you and taking you shopping until you max out your credit card."

"Because you're hoping I'll be depressed enough to buy you some new shoes."

"There is that."

"We can drop this. I need to be a grownup. We never agreed to contact each other."

"Who are you trying to convince?"

She was silent for a moment. Then, because she knew Margot would ferret out the information anyway, Brandy admitted, "He invited me to a party at the Moline."

"Ha! I knew there was more to the story. You turned him down and broke his heart and you want me to take your side, so you make it sound like he dumped you on your ass."

"That's not the way it is."

"No guy would willingly put up with me unless he was really into you. Argue with that."

"I got nothing," Brandy said with a laugh.

"He's not like Reyes," Margot said. "Not that I'm taking his side or anything."

"And not that you like him."

"Never will. Go with him. He's already fucked you and beat you, how much worse can it get?"

"When you put it that way..."

"Call me," Margot said. "I could use a margarita at Teddy's Lodge. Or some retail therapy on your card. Or, better yet, invite that pirate to come with us."

"Gregorio?"

"Swoon."

"You think BDSM demeans participants," she reminded her friend.

"Maybe I should be more open-minded. He has an earring. Can you imagine him with an eye patch?" With that, she was gone.

Every fifteen minutes throughout the morning, Brandy checked her phone. No calls. No texts. No emails. It was as if the damned thing had lost service.

Then, mid-afternoon, a delivery van arrived.

She frowned as she signed for the large, odd-shaped package. There was no return address on the box, and she took it inside and sliced through the packaging tape. Two more boxes were inside the first. She opened the smallest one to find a human-sized rubber foot inside. "Oh my God." She gasped and laughed. "I think this is for you." She gave the toy to MW.

Dana looked at the smaller dog then the foot, then she backed away. MW attacked the rubber toes as if they were an enemy.

The next box was heavy, and it contained a gigantic bone. Dana started sniffing and strolled over. "You didn't get left out," she said, putting the thing on the floor.

As she went to throw away the box, something else caught her eye. A soft toy turtle, coloured bright blue and green, lay on the bottom. She pulled it out, along with a tube of catnip. Whisper began his unholy cries and rolled onto his back. And that was before she filled the turtle. "I think you can have this one outside."

After she took the toy and the cardboard outside, she came in to find her phone had a received a text message.

Is my bribe working?

She pressed the phone to her chest. Goofy, ridiculous, fabulous man. Using her pets to get to her?

The burst of energy that shot through her after hearing from him carried her through the rest of the afternoon, and she met every one of her deadlines.

The next time her phone chimed, the message was from Margot.

Margaritas?

She tapped out a quick reply, saying he'd sent a rubber foot to MW.

The man tolerates me and that little monster? He's a saint.

The next day he sent her a short but demure black dress. In the right size.

He'd included a short note.

I booked us a room at the hotel.

On Wednesday a pair of heels arrived.

She tried on the outfit and stared at herself in the mirror, looking for flaws. Even though she was her own worst critic, she had to admit he'd chosen well. That first night at the Den, she'd worn a black dress, and the material had clung to her curves. This one flowed over her body. The neckline would reveal the barest hint of cleavage. And if they danced, the dress would move with her. It was perfect.

Through his website, she sent him an email, complaining that he didn't play fair.

The bastard didn't respond.

Thursday's delivery of lingerie pushed her over the edge. Stockings, a garter belt, a bra, even panties were nestled in layers of tissue paper.

She would have expected him to demand she wear nothing beneath the dress. The fact he'd realised she'd get a confidence boost from attending as his date rather than as a submissive spoke volumes to her.

An hour after the delivery, he finally called.

She stared at his name on the caller identification screen for a few seconds, resisting the impulse to answer on the first ring. The dogs jumped up and barked, adding to her racing heart. She shushed the animals. Dana settled right away. MW continued to turn in crazy, loud circles. Maybe a break from this wouldn't be all bad.

Right before her phone would switch him over to voicemail, she answered. "You are relentless," she said by way of greeting.

"I gave you fair warning."

She sank onto a kitchen chair.

"I've missed you this week," he continued.

His voice curled through her like the ribbons he'd used on his packages. Rough, gruff, but somehow refined at the same time. The contrast drew her closer and closer.

"Tell me you missed me, too."

She'd been raised by her father, and he'd protected her. She hadn't been allowed to date until she was almost ready to graduate from high school. Her first serious relationship had been with a guy named Sam, and he'd introduced her to BDSM. Not that she'd needed a long courtship with his lash or pleasing him. He'd been drunk on power, and he'd used kink as a way to get her to do all the chores, cooking, cleaning and taking care of him at the expense of her own success.

Gregorio had set her straight on that.

Too bad Reyes had reinforced Sam's message.

"Tell me you missed me, too," Master Niles urged.

"I missed you." And she had. Now that she'd admitted it, the reality of it rushed in. All week, she'd tried to keep the feelings at bay. She knew Margot and Gregorio worried about her, and truthfully, she did, too. Despite her reassurances to her friends, she knew she was susceptible to the power that Doms exuded. Her need to protect herself was at odds with her need to care and nurture others. As Master Niles had surmised, there was a reason she had a houseful of abandoned animals.

"I can't endure tomorrow night unless you're there. I'm throwing myself on your mercy. Take pity on me."

She laughed. "There's not a more competent man on the planet, Sir. But you win."

"Brandy, if I do what I'm supposed to, there will be no doubt in your mind you're the one who won. You've got my undying gratitude."

No doubt she was falling for him. Her heart was still racing, and the idea of being at the event with him sent adrenaline spikes through her. To diminish some of the impacts, she paced the floor.

MW dived for her toes. She scooped up his rubber foot and tossed it into the living room, sending him skidding after it. For this toy alone, she loved Master Niles.

"I can drive up to get you," he said.

"That's ridiculous, Sir."

"I don't want to ask you to make the drive by yourself."

"The weather forecast is clear."

"You checked?"

Several times over the last twenty-four hours.

"When did I have you?" he asked. "Was it the dress?"

"It was the rubber foot, Sir. It will save my pedicures."

"I knew it. The dress fits?"

"As if it were made for me."

"It was altered for you."

She stopped pacing to collapse against the refrigerator.

"If you change your mind, I'm happy to come and get you. Otherwise, if you want to arrive around noon, the hotel has a spa."

"That's a little outside my budget, Sir."

"It's part of the package deal with the room. It includes hair styling, manicure, pedicure, facial, massage. Hell, there's stuff on this brochure I've never heard of. Hot stones? Some of it scares me a little. I'd hate to see them go to waste."

She wondered if she could leave right now.

"Are your pets taken care of? Or do I need to find someone?"

Her heart melted. "I can get a neighbour. We help each other out."

"Your work schedule is clear?"

"There are a couple of private functions at the Den this weekend. I'm not due in until Sunday night."

"Perfect. Let me know when you're on your way. Oh, and Brandy? My cock's been hard since I left you. I can't wait to be buried in you."

Now it was the only thing she could think of.

After finishing her work, she took the dogs for a walk to burn off some energy. She stopped by her neighbour's house rather than calling him and made arrangements for him to care for the house.

"When will you be back?" Martin asked.

"I'll let you know if I need you to look in Saturday night or Sunday morning." Her fingers were secretly crossed that she wouldn't be back until Sunday. That was presumptuous, though.

That evening, she showered before going to bed with her vibrator.

Her fantasies were of Master Niles and the last time they'd gone to bed together. While there was never a doubt he was a Dom, the scene had had a decidedly erotic, rather than BDSM edge. He hadn't restrained her in any way. Rather, he'd had her on all fours and driven into her, but then stayed still. Instead of it being a raw, physical act, the connection had given space for emotion to add to the dynamic. She'd felt closer to him during that act than at any other time.

She turned up the setting on the vibrator and rubbed it over her clit, remembering the pulse of his cock deep inside her, the feel of his hands on her body, the scent of power and restraint that had stamped the air.

With a cry, she jerked, lifting her pelvis, thinking about him and pressing the vibrator hard against her throbbing pussy. Her orgasm crashed over her.

Out of breath, she flicked off the switch and dropped the wand.

She closed her eyes and tried to settle. But she couldn't. Restless energy gnawed at her.

All night, she tossed and turned, wishing away the hours.

The next morning, as coffee dripped into the carafe with agonising slowness, she realised she was so keyed up about seeing him that she'd forgotten to be nervous about the event.

Her phone rang before seven. This time when she saw his name appear, she didn't even pretend to be an ice princess. She answered on the first ring.

"Sorry if I woke you," he said.

"I didn't sleep much," she replied.

"You will tonight after a good workout."

And in his arms. She rubbed a bare arm with her hand.

"I should have waited to hear from you," he said. "But I couldn't."

"I'm glad."

"Do you know when you're leaving?"

"I have some work I want to finish up and a couple of loads of laundry to do. Around eleven, I hope."

"I'll count the hours."

She wondered where he was. Home? An office? She wanted to be able to picture him in his surroundings, and she wondered if she'd have the opportunity. He hadn't invited her to his house, and she told herself that was okay. They didn't have a relationship. This was simply an overnight date. She was doing a favour for a friend.

Too bad she couldn't make her heart listen to her head.

"Remember to call when you're on your way. You know where you're going and how to get there? The entrance for valet parking is off Champa Street."

"I've already programmed my GPS, Sir," she assured him. After they'd said their goodbyes, she grabbed a mug from a cupboard. Impatience made her grateful the coffee maker had the feature that allowed her to pull out the carafe and pour a cup without making a mess all over the countertop.

She carried her drink into her office and powered up her computer, intending to force herself to work if necessary. No way would she spend the morning obsessing about the upcoming fundraiser.

An hour later, she realised she wasn't fooling anyone. She was staring out of the window more than she was getting anything done. Giving up, she refreshed her coffee, tossed a load of laundry in the washing machine then dressed in a skirt with tights. She added her favourite cocoa-coloured suede boots and a turtleneck sweater. Suitable for the hotel lobby, she hoped.

She managed to focus long enough to make some final notes on Master Niles' website and logo redesign.

Then she fed the lizards and cleaned their tank before walking the dogs and checking on Whisper. Since he'd been given the catnip, he had periods of great energy where he moved like a blur in her peripheral vision followed by long naps. The toy had to be an every once in a while treat, she decided.

By nine, her bag was packed. She had all her makeup, two curling irons, three brushes and the gifts Master Niles had sent. She added an extra outfit, just in case.

An hour earlier than planned, she was ready to leave.

When she turned onto the main road from her neighbourhood, she called him. "I'm on my way."

"Good. I'll meet you in the lobby."

The sky was a stunning, winter blue. No clouds obscured the sun. The roads were clear and dry, with light traffic.

She stopped for a vanilla latte in Frisco. Since she didn't get to town often, it was a rare treat. If she sipped, it would last most of the way to Denver.

When she left the foothills and headed for the plains, she realised she should have asked for a decaf. As it was, she'd drunk most of a pot of coffee before leaving home.

She turned on the radio to distract herself, but she still gripped the steering wheel with white knuckles.

As she approached I-25, she turned off the radio so she could pay attention to the driving directions.

Master Niles had said he'd meet her in the lobby, but he was waiting in the valet area.

Her heart stopped. He stood under the portico near the revolving glass door, one foot propped on the wall behind him, arms folded across his chest.

She knew the moment he recognised her.

He pushed off and strode towards her car, devastating in a black cashmere sweater, black trousers and polished black shoes. He looked part rogue, part corporate executive, all movie-star handsome.

The valet opened her door and handed her a claim ticket, before Master Niles said, "If you'll have her luggage sent to fourteen-oh-seven?"

"Of course, Mr Malloy."

He tipped the man before kissing her forehead. "Welcome to Denver."

"I'm glad to be here, Sir."

With his fingertips at the small of her back, he guided her towards the revolving door.

"Let's get you settled," he said. "I hope you don't mind, I had some snacks sent to the room and booked you in for a well-deserved pedicure after a massage. If you want to add anything else, feel free."

"That all sounds delightful." Once they were in the brass elevator and the doors shut, she turned to him. "But a round of hot, sweaty sex sounds even better."

He pushed her against the back of the car, pinning her hands above her head and using a knee to prise apart her thighs. "A woman after my own heart." He lifted the hem of her skirt with his free hand and worked his way beneath her tights and panties to dip two fingers into her suddenly damp pussy. "Mine," he said, voice gruff against her ear, making her nerves tingle. "Have you been playing with yourself, Ms Hess?"

"Of course, Sir. Fantasising about you."

He finger-fucked her, fast, deep, relentless. He knew what she needed, and he gave it to her...the certainty that he wanted her as badly as she wanted him, the promise of more to come, the unspoken assurance that she mattered to him. When he bit her neck, she whimpered and went limp, coming all over his hand.

The elevator dinged in advance of its arrival at the fourteenth floor.

He pulled out and straightened her skirt. "That ought to hold you for a few minutes?" He licked his fingers.

She blinked, hardly able to believe that had just happened.

The car stopped and the doors slid open. "After you."

He led her down the carpeted hall. In front of fourteen-oh-seven, he pulled out two electronic keys. He gave her one and opened the door with the other. "I checked them both," he said.

The suite was sumptuous, with floor-to-ceiling windows with a view of the Rockies and three separate rooms. The large living room held a couch, chair and coffee table all facing the wall-mounted television. The a wet bar had pendant lighting above it, each glass globe painted in an explosion of primary colours.

On the marble surface, a champagne bottle was chilling in a silver ice bucket. Two crystal flutes stood invitingly off to one side.

A wheeled serving cart was parked nearby, and she could see plates filled with chocolates, scones, vegetables, dip, crackers and cheese.

"I call this a feast, not a snack, Sir." And to think she'd almost opted to stay home and eat leftovers. "I may never leave," she told him.

"We could arrange that."

She laughed. "A month here would cost my entire year's salary. And the dogs would be hell on the hardwood."

"Maybe an occasional visit, then," he said.

A knock on the door interrupted them, and the bellwoman brought in Brandy's bag.

"We shouldn't be bothered again. How hungry are you?"

"For what, Sir?"

"Good answer."

He led her towards the bar and she gathered his intent. "Finishing what you started in the elevator?" she asked.

His eyes had darkened.

Feminine fascination unfurled through her.

This far above the ground with no other skyscrapers near, they'd be away from voyeuristic eyes.

He pulled off her shirt while she stripped from the waist down.

He undressed with a frantic energy she relished. Their clothes fell in untidy heaps.

"Hold onto the bar."

She heard, rather than saw him grab a condom from a pocket. He ripped open the package and dropped it on the floor. She knew him to be restrained and thoughtful, so his lack of control thrilled her. "Do me," she said. "I'm still wet for you."

"On your toes."

Because of their height difference, he had to bend his knees, and he parted her buttocks.

He took her in one stroke that pitched her forward and made her gasp. "Sir!"

"I've thought about you all week."

"I've been craving this," she confessed, her whole body on fire.

He pumped his dick in her, almost pulling all the way out before surging with unleashed power.

Being fourteen floors up, looking at the mountains, made the whole thing surreal. Even if they didn't see each other after this, even if her heart was in a million pieces when their affair ended, this moment was worth the risk.

He reached around to toy with her clit, and she balanced on the edge of an orgasm.

"Are you close already?"

"Sir, I've been like this every hour of the day for the entire week."

"Good."

He pinched her clit.

The exquisite pain made her jerk, and he moved forward at the same time, impaling her on his dick.

He turned her head and captured her mouth in an awkward kiss that swallowed her scream.

She trembled and shook.

"Squeeze my dick with your pussy," he said.

Still riding her orgasm, she somehow managed to do what he commanded. His arms went around her like steel bands, holding her still. After a few thrusts, he froze. Then he shuddered, ejaculating his load with a grunt of pure, male satisfaction.

Surprising her, he held onto her for a long moment, resting his head against hers. She'd never had any man—Dom or not—engage in this kind of intimacy after sex. She wished the moment could last forever.

His flaccid cock slid out, then he picked her up and carried her from the room.

"If you keep doing this, I'm going to forget how to walk, Sir."

"As long as you can crawl when I want you to, it's fine with me."

She grinned, turning towards him.

"Do you want a shower or to freshen up? We've got a bidet."

"A bidet?" she asked. "Really?"

"For freshening up," he warned her. "This weekend, your orgasms belong to me."

"Yes, Sir," she agreed, kissing his cheek.

The bathroom was another treat, with its clean lines, art deco inspired tile floor, double sinks, designer faucets, tub and shower and private water closet. He set her down and she adjusted the bidet's water.

"Are you going to watch?" she asked.

"I am."

It shouldn't bother her. They'd had anal sex, she'd submitted to him, he'd brought her off in the elevator. But this, with him looking at her as if there were no one else in the world, unnerved her.

Knowing he wanted this gave her all the courage she needed to straddle the bidet and wash herself in the stream of warm water.

"Let me help," he said, squatting next to her and parting her labia.

His touch and the jet on her swollen pussy were dizzying. She began to sway as arousal unfurled in her.

"You've got a gorgeous pussy, Brandy."

She didn't respond. She was lost…

"I think you like this."

"*Yes.*"

Abruptly he released her and shut off the water.

"What?" She opened her eyes in time to see him grab a hand towel and offer it to her. "Sir," she protested.

"You've had a week of deciding when to come. Today, tomorrow, I choose. I think I've already been generous." He raised his eyebrows in question.

"More than, Sir," she agreed, remembering her place. Master Niles wasn't an ordinary man, he was an unremitting Dom. "Thank you."

"Much better."

He helped her to stand, and she was grateful for the support.

"There's a robe in the wardrobe," he told her. "Feel free to wear that while we have lunch. Would you like a glass of champagne?"

"Please." Because of her relationship with Reyes, she wasn't gaga over finer things like she used to be, but this, on a Friday afternoon, seemed decadent.

While he turned on the shower, she went into the bedroom.

The eclectic décor continued there. Geometric black and white patterns were interrupted by splashes of vibrant red. She'd never be bold enough to try a palette like this, but she loved the way it came together.

She unpacked and hung up her dress next to the tuxedo he had hanging in the wardrobe. Her mouth watered at the idea of seeing him in it. On so many different levels, he appealed to her, and this was just one more to add to the dynamic fire he lit in her. At least for tonight, he was all hers.

Brandy wrapped herself in a robe then went into the living room. Two glasses were filled with champagne, and she picked up one. Then, realising she hadn't eaten anything at all today, took a piece of cheese that had a toothpick sticking out of it.

She stood near the window, admiring the view. She enjoyed a piece of cheddar then sipped from the flute of bubbly and wondered if life could possibly get any better.

Then it did.

"You're more delicious than the chocolate," Master Niles said, walking towards her with only a towel wrapped around his lean hips.

"I started without you. I apologise."

"Don't." He picked up a glass and tilted it towards her.

"To you, Sir," she said.

"To us," he replied, clinking the rims together.

They each took a sip then he filled a plate for her with various cheeses, crackers, vegetables and dip.

"You're spoiling me."

"You deserve it."

She slid onto a chair at the bar, and he sat next to her.

"Thank you for being here."

"When you get the credit card bill, you might not be so pleased with yourself."

"I think I will."

A cherry tomato halfway to her mouth, she paused. He was looking at her with those all-knowing hazel eyes. And she knew he meant what he said.

"Your massage is at two," he said. "Don't worry about the bill or the tip. It's been taken care of."

"Really, Sir—"

"Please." He placed a finger on her lips. "Let me."

"I don't want to feel like I owe you."

"This is pre-payment," he said. "You're going to earn this."

"Your aunt is that horrible?"

"Worse than you can imagine." He shuddered.

She laughed and popped the tomato in her mouth. "Can I bill stuff to the room?" She glanced at the tray. "As ominous as that sounds, I may need more chocolate."

He brushed his fingertips across her jaw bone. "Anything you want, Brandy."

"Anything?" She glanced at his towel.

"Especially that."

When she reached for him, he captured her hand. "Later."

She sighed.

"I have work to do and you have a massage and pedicure scheduled. Insatiable wench."

After checking the clock, she excused herself to get dressed.

"I'll see you back here for cocktails," he said.

Confusing her, he kissed her before she left the room. It would be so easy to think they had a relationship, so easy to believe...

* * * *

She spent the afternoon being pampered and telling herself not to fall in love with Master Niles while alternately praying it wasn't already too late.

When she returned to the room, her body feeling like melted butter from the massage, he was on the phone.

He raised a hand, promising to be with her soon.

Captivated by this new side of him, she looked at him for a moment. Wearing wool slacks as he had earlier, this man didn't at all resemble the Niles who'd cooked burgers at her house. Nor would anyone recognise him as the Dom who put subs into the direst bondage imaginable on video.

As he spoke on the phone, his tones were clipped, not at all like anything she'd ever heard from him.

With her, with subs, he could be gruff. With the people at her party, he'd been conversational. But now, he sounded as if he wanted to buy a country.

Giving him a quick smile, and not wanting to be guilty of eavesdropping, she indicated that she was going to take a bath.

When he walked in, she was soaking up to her chin, feeling grateful the hot water heater hadn't run out like it might have at her house.

"Mind if I join you?"

It hadn't taken her long to learn there was no such thing as privacy with this Dom. If she were truthful with herself, she'd admit that was one of the things she enjoyed about this kind of interaction.

"You do know what day this is?"

"Friday," she said. "Why?"

"We talked about you bathing me becoming a Friday night ritual."

"We did. And if you want me to, Sir, of course I will."

"But you look too relaxed to move."

"It's your fault for treating me like a princess."

"I'll treat you like something different later," he said.

"I'm honestly not sure I've ever been this relaxed in my entire life, Sir."

"I'd say you've earned it. Can I get you another champagne?"

"Only if you want my undying gratitude."

"I'll take that as a yes." He produced a glass from behind his back.

"You're full of tricks, Master Niles." With a squeal of delight, she accepted it and took a sip.

"And now," he said dramatically, "for my next trick…"

He dropped the towel. His cock was erect, and it made her suck in a breath. "That's hardly a trick, Master Niles. It seems like it's more of an everyday occurrence. Maybe every hour."

"A little appreciation, if you please, Your Majesty?"

"It's impressive, even if it happens all the time," she said with a giggle.

Proving he was full of surprises, he left the room for a minute before returning with a glass for himself. Then he climbed into the tub with her.

"You don't have work to do?" she asked, moving to make room for him.

"Nothing is more important than you." He took a drink from the flute he'd brought for himself. "How was your afternoon?"

"Amazing, Sir. Yours?"

"Glad you were here waiting when I finished that call."

"Frustrating?" she asked.

"Amazingly. I had information on my website, or at least I thought I did, and my potential client couldn't find it."

"A few days ago, I sent you an email through your website. Thanking you, letting you know you were wearing me down."

"If it had been working correctly, I would have responded."

"You could let your webmaster know you have an issue."

"I think I just did."

"I…" She blinked. "What?"

"Write up a contract. You're hired."

"You're—"

"Serious," he finished. "Yes I am."

"You don't know my price." If she weren't in the tub, she'd be doing a jig in the bathroom. That wouldn't be professional, but then again, neither was negotiating a deal in the bathtub.

"I saw your mock-ups. I think I told you I was impressed not only with what you did, but the fact you took the initiative."

She tried not to squeal. Adding his company to her résumé would give her some much-needed credentials.

"Red."

She blinked. "Red?"

"Betting you chose red for your toenails."

"How in the hell do you do that? Juggle twenty things in your mind at once? And I take it that's the end of the business discussion."

"Am I right?"

She lifted her right leg.

"With a flower on the big toe. I wouldn't have guessed that."

"Do you like it?" She looked at him, trying to gauge his reaction. "I hope you do. You paid for it."

"Ms Hess, no matter what you chose, it would have been perfect."

Instead of letting her emotions spiral out of control, she reined them in and asked, "Is your aunt really that bad?"

He took a drink. "This has nothing to do with Mame." He took Brandy's flute and set both glasses aside before pulling her against his chest.

She was straddling him, and she felt his erection. Brandy expected him to enter her, and she would have liked that, but he didn't. Instead, he held her. In the moment, she felt safe, protected, as if the two of them could take on the world—folly, her practical side warned. She could make her own way in the world, and how foolish would it be to fall for a man who'd sworn never again to risk his heart?

"I'm glad you're here," he said.

"Me too."

"As much as I'd like to hold you all day, we're expected to meet my aunt."

Reluctantly she eased away.

He climbed from the tub first and offered a towel to her. When she refused it, he grinned. His expression turned to a frown when she wrapped herself in the robe again.

"I'd keep you naked if I could."

"Chained to a wall?"

"Could work."

She laughed.

Niles excused himself to answer a few emails, returning ten minutes later with the champagne. He topped off her glass while she styled her hair.

"I'll be honest," he said. "I wanted to look at you."

She tilted her glass towards him in acknowledgement. "Now, Sir, get out of here, otherwise we'll be late."

"At this point, I'm willing to take the risk."

"Out," she said, closing the door behind him.

Half an hour later, she smoothed down the dress then slipped into the stilettos and joined him in the living area.

From his place by the window, backlit by the setting sun, he looked up.

His jacket hung from one of the bar stools, and the sleeves of his white shirt were turned back. The ends of his tie hung loose. He looked dashing in his dishevelled state.

"Turn around," he said.

Slowly, she did so, the material swaying with her movement.

When she faced him, he said, "Stunning. Everything I imagined and more." He held out a hand and she went to him. "Thank you," he said, kissing her hand.

She lowered her gaze then glanced up at him through her lashes. "No, Sir. Thank *you*. For everything."

"I have one more gift for you this evening," he said.

"You've done too much as it is, Sir. I can't possibly —"

"Indulge me." He released her hand and went behind the bar.

He returned carrying a jeweller's box.

"Sir, really, I can't accept anything else."

"Open it," he said, voice brooking no argument. "I hope you like it."

Her heart stopped as she took it from him and removed the lid. A silver necklace lay there, its pendant a circle. She immediately recognised its significance. Friends and acquaintances who knew him as Master Niles would also garner its meaning. Others, though, would think it was a stylish piece of jewellery. "Master Niles, I'm speechless."

"Thank you is the customary response when you receive a gift," he said wryly.

"It's more than a gift," she said. It wasn't a collar. It wasn't gold. And there were no diamonds.

"It will look beautiful with the dress."

"You're right about that." The neckline called out for adornment, and now she realised why he'd selected this particular dress.

"It doesn't have to mean anything more than you want it to. It's a stunning accessory. It also says you're with me. I want you to know how much you mean to me. And I want you to wear it, but I'll understand if you choose not to."

With him standing so close, she could hardly think. She ached to feel its weight on her, but was worried about its implications if she agreed to wear it. He'd never suggested they make their relationship anything more than friendship, and even if he did, she couldn't dare accept.

"What do you say, Brandy?"

C h a p t e r S e v e n

Niles watched different reactions cross her face. When he'd offered the box, she'd kept her hand at her side, making a fist. He'd hoped for delight or joy, not suspicion.

Then when she'd seen the necklace, she'd started to smile, but the expression had faded as she'd taken in its shape.

Niles had selected the piece with great care. When he'd entered the jeweller's, he'd been uncertain what he was looking for, just something suitable to go with the dress. When he'd seen that particular necklace, nothing else would do.

He was a Dom. Nothing would change that. Call it passion or possession. She was with him tonight, and he wanted to be sure everyone knew it. Although it wasn't a collar—he'd never collar a sub again—it did have multiple meanings.

He waited. Her response mattered more than he'd thought it might.

She traced the circle then she looked up at him, her finger still on the silver. "It's beautiful. Thank you."

Ridiculously pleased, he picked it up. This part, he had imagined.

All week, he'd thought about seeing her again. If this event hadn't been on his calendar, he'd have invented something. Even if she wasn't a crack web designer, he would have hired her as a reason to stay in contact.

Her house was crazy with noise and activity. In contrast, the walls in his home had echoed with loneliness.

She lifted her hair, and he fastened the clasp. "Perfect," he told her when she turned to show it off. "Better than I imagined. And I imagined plenty."

Together they took the elevator to the lobby, and were among the first to arrive.

The hotel didn't have a specific ballroom. Instead, the main floor served as the party space. There were plenty of alcoves for silent auction items and a large, open area for mingling. A band was warming up in what was generally the bar, and a space had been cleared for dancing. Tables were triangular in shape, rather than round. Chair backs were short. Tall glass vases filled with flowers sat next to shorter, squat ones. Everything was a visual feast.

"This isn't what I expected," she said.

"Is it pretentious enough for you, though?"

"I apologise if I was a brat. This is fabulous. Exactly my style."

"Which is quirky?"

She wrinkled her nose.

"Bold?"

"Yes."

"Fun?

"All of that," she responded with a laugh. She leaned into him and pressed her palm against his chest, on his heart. "You're not so bad yourself."

"If you see something we need to bid on, let me know."

"Denver Nuggets tickets, if they have them."

"You like basketball?" He couldn't have been more shocked if she'd asked for tickets to outer space.

"Doesn't everyone?"

"No. In fact, some people can't stand it."

"Fine, if we win them, I'll take Margot to the game." She grinned.

"On second thought, I like basketball just fine."

His aunt spotted them and hurried over. "Incoming," he warned Brandy. "And she's a bit like you, in that she speaks what's on her mind."

"I adore her already," Brandy said.

"I was afraid of that."

Tall and thin to the point of being gaunt, Aunt Mame wore a long, cream-coloured sequined gown that plunged in the back. She shimmered and shone, and teetered on four-inch heels. Her short silver hair was spiked and held in place by some gravity-defying feat. She had eyes only for Brandy, and her bright red lips were parted in a genuine smile.

Now that he saw Auntie Mame, he was glad he came. When he'd first lost Eleanor, Mame's vibrant energy had been hard to take, but now it was infectious.

He expected a hug or for her to present her cheek for a quick kiss, but she ignored him and swept Brandy into her arms. "Hello, luv. Thank you, thank you." She stepped back and held Brandy by the upper arms. "I've been dying to look at you. Beautiful. My gawd, that hair."

"Aunt Mame, meet Brandy Hess. She's a web designer and she—"

175

"Yes, yes, we can get to that later. The only thing that matters is she got you out of the house and to my party. She could be on the police blotter for all I care. In fact, hiding her in the kitchen when the coppers show up could be fun."

Brandy laughed.

"Brandy, meet my incorrigible auntie."

Mame spared him a glance. "Why don't you be a good boy and fetch us a glass of something while we get to know one another?"

"Brandy, say the word and I'll rescue you from my aunt's well-meaning, but nosy questions."

"I'm parched," she replied.

"Run along," Mame said, in the same tone she might have used when he was ten years old.

He held up his hands. "Two-to-one. I can't win."

"Off you go," Mame said.

He headed for the bar and began to feel as if there was a conspiracy. The bartender took his time finding a bottle, uncorking it then pulling out glasses, lining them up in a precise row. He chatted about the upcoming Denver Broncos game and told him they'd be televising it if he was ever downtown and wanted to watch it away from the usual sports bars. Which made him think of Brandy and her short kilt.

That was he point the stopped listening to the man.

When Niles drew out his wallet to pay, the bartender waved him off, saying champagne was included in the price of the tickets. Niles left a nice tip, mostly because of the image of Brandy bending over in that tartan skirt.

By the time he found the ladies, his name was the first on at least six bids sheets, getting things rolling. With luck, he wouldn't win them all. But if he did,

Brandy would be happy. He supposed that made it a no-lose situation.

"Brandy's going to take a look at one of my websites," Mame said.

"Indeed?"

Mame held up her smart phone. Her home page was displayed on the screen. There were some funky words and symbols displayed. "I thought I knew how to do all that myself, but I obviously did some things wrong. This dear girl said she could have them all fixed by Monday, and she had the idea to acknowledge tonight's winners and thank all the donors, linking to each person's site as a way to draw more traffic."

"All that happened in five minutes?" he asked.

"No. All that happened in less than one minute," Mame corrected. "I spent the other four grilling her about your relationship. She changed the subject. Smart and socially astute. Well done," she told him. "Hold onto her, Niles, my boy."

She patted his cheek before excusing herself to hone in on new arrivals.

"Whew," Brandy said. "She has more energy than I've had in my entire life."

Waitstaff brought around canapés, and Brandy bit into a crab cheese wonton with great gusto, another thing he appreciated about her. It wasn't just with food, it was everything. Her sunny outlook gave him new appreciation.

He got caught up talking to an associate, and he saw Brandy out of the corner of his eye, chatting with a couple who used to be friends with Eleanor. She seemed relaxed, interested in the conversation.

Throughout the evening, he saw her touching her necklace, and every time, he had a visceral response.

He wondered what it might be like if she was his. Though he'd sworn never to fall in love again, that didn't stop him from imagining.

The band struck up a love song, providing him the perfect opportunity to hold her. He went in search of her, seeing her chatting with a tall, broad man. She was leaning towards him, obviously engaged in a discussion.

She dazzled him with a one thousand watt smile when he walked up. Her reaction left no doubt she was here with him. "This is Marvin Jones. He's looking for investors for his start-up electric vehicle company. Not cars. Something else entirely. It might be a good fit for you, but I told Mr Jones that he'd need to schedule an appointment with you."

"Indeed?" More and more, this woman was getting to him. She hadn't been flirting with the guy, she had been talking business—his business. And she hadn't promised he'd speak to this Jones fellow, she'd been protecting his time. "If Brandy thinks it's worthwhile us talking, I'm happy to meet with you." He gave the gentleman one of his business cards. "Now, if you'll excuse us, I'd like to dance with my woman."

He guided her towards the dance floor. "How long before we can excuse ourselves?" he asked as she wove her hands around his neck and placed her cheek on his lapel. The way she had greeted him with her genuine smile had made it clear he was the only man in the room she was interested in.

"I'm ready to go anytime you are, Sir," she said.

When the dance had ended, Mame took the microphone. She thanked everyone for coming, then turned over the event to the people she'd hired to hype the silent auction. Over the next couple of hours, the items were described with Hollywood flair. And the donors were acknowledged and asked to take a bow.

He and Brandy stayed until the end. He did win her the basketball tickets. No doubt he could have bought the team for less money.

"The research society thanks you," Mame said.

"And so do I," Brandy added.

"You have to wear a kilt to the game," he told her.

"Sir, I'd do anything for you."

"Told you she's a keeper," Mame said, moving off with no apparent loss of energy.

"That was a joke," he clarified when they were in the elevator.

"What was?"

"The kilt. I'm not letting you out in public dressed like that."

"I could wear white stockings with it."

"Put me out of my misery."

"Here?" she asked, sliding her hand towards his crotch. "Now?"

"Good God, no."

"Just thought I'd ask, Sir."

When they returned to the room, she finished what she'd started. She unfastened his belt and trousers, then said, "Commando, Sir?" before sliding to her knees and taking his cock into her warm mouth.

She sucked him off, and he had her head trapped between his palms.

After their shared shower, he licked her cunt until she screamed, then she fell asleep in his arms.

When he awoke in the middle of the night, he pulled her against him.

When dawn lit the mountains, she was still there. Because of her breathing, he knew she was awake. "Go home with me?"

"I'd love to, Sir."

They joined a jubilant Mame for breakfast and coffee.

"Congratulations on a successful event," Brandy said. "I'll be sure to email you with those suggestions so you can keep some momentum going."

"Do you mind just going ahead and doing the work? My assistant can give you logins and whatnot. I emailed her your information and told her to get you the attendee list and the donor list. You'll also get a list of all the winners. I'll leave you two to sort it all out. I've decided to take a trip to Belize for a little R & R," she said. Grinning, she added, "With Truex Williams."

"Isn't that a little sudden?"

"Spur of the moment."

Niles sat back and drummed his fingers on the table. "Truex Williams is thirty years younger than you are. At least."

"Thirty-five. But who's counting? But at least he can keep up with me and none of the old farts my age can. I need some good loving," she said. "From a man who can keep it up all night."

"Bleach! I need bleach for my ears." Niles groaned. "Too much information."

"Pish. Like you two didn't go at it like rabbits last night." Over the rim of her mimosa, Mame regarded Brandy.

"I've no idea what you're talking about, ma'am." Brandy poured a splash of cream into her coffee. "I went upstairs and fell asleep."

Mame nodded then wagged a finger at Niles. "This one's definitely a keeper."

He was beginning to think the same thing.

After Mame had excused herself, he and Brandy packed their bags. She followed him to his loft, which wasn't more than two miles away. He directed her to his garage while he parked under the carport.

"I had no idea you were so close. We could have stayed here," she said.

"I wanted to spoil you."

"I appreciate it."

His place was wide open, industrial-looking with exposed brick and duct work. It was constructed from light wood, stainless steel, tall windows, lots of stunning lighting and not much else.

"No artwork, Sir?"

"I've never gotten around to it."

"No photographs? Mementos? I gather you didn't live here with your wife?"

"My aunt isn't the only one who's nosy."

"You can always refuse to answer or put your tongue in my mouth to shut me up," she said lightly, though her brows were drawn together.

He didn't respond right away, and she walked towards the window, her back to him.

"This must be difficult for you," he said. She obviously wanted to get to know him better, and she had that right. But when she asked questions, she was treading on uncertain ground. "It's not easy for me, either." He joined her at the window. "I'm not accustomed to talking about it, about her." Wryly, he added, "Most people have respected that. Except you and Aunt Mame."

"Sorry, Sir. I guess you could order me not to mention her again, and I will honour that. But I think that changes our dynamic, puts boundaries around it. In that case, I understand where you're coming from."

He took her by the shoulders and drew her towards him. "I wouldn't have invited you to my place if I had wanted to keep you out of my personal life."

"Then you'll have to put up with my inquisitiveness."

"I suppose I will."

"Is it a hardship, Sir?"

"At times, yes," he admitted. He used both of his hands to brush hair back from her face. "But you're worth it."

"Thank you."

"And no, I never lived here with Eleanor."

"It's obvious. Not to be insulting, but your space doesn't have a woman's touch. It seems as if you hired someone, or you looked online and picked out a style from a home magazine and ordered everything they suggested."

He was a man accustomed to being in charge, confident. But he let her go and shifted uncomfortably. "You're right. I hired someone. I never saw this place before I bought it. My real estate agent put our house on the market, arranged for the sale of all our personal belongings and found me this loft. You're the first person to visit me here."

She curled her hand into his T-shirt. "Shall we make some memories?"

In his bedroom, they did.

* * * *

He took her to dinner at a loud place on the Sixteenth Street Mall. They sat on the patio, drank ridiculously large beers from glasses that resembled fishbowls and watched people pass by. "Did you make arrangements for someone to take care of the Hess Zoo?"

"Thank you, yes. I called my neighbour while you were in the shower earlier." She took a drink, needing both hands to lift it up. "Thank you for the concern. I'm free until mid-morning then I have to get back in time to go to work at the Den."

He nodded, feeling more uncomfortable with that idea than he might have imagined. He wanted Brandy on her knees, but greeting him. He didn't have the right to ask that of her, but that didn't mean he wasn't tempted.

"There's a store in Larimer Square I'd like to stop in on the way back, if you don't mind?"

"Anything in particular you're looking for?"

"Candles. For your place, Sir. Unless that's too presumptuous?"

"Not at all."

After dinner, they walked back up the mall, dodging pedestrians and stopping to watch a woman who created charcoal caricatures in less than two minutes.

"I want one of us," Brandy said.

"Are you serious?"

"Do you ever do anything spontaneous?"

"No."

"You do now, Sir," she said, taking a twenty dollar bill out of her wallet.

The artist directed Brandy to sit on a stool, and he stood behind her.

With a few dozen, economic yet bold strokes and blurring the lines with the heel of her hand, the woman created a portrait that captured his expression — happier than it had been in years, and yet pensive at the same time.

The piece of paper rolled, wrapped in a rubber band and safely tucked inside her purse, they headed for the shop in Larimer Square.

She picked out a couple of candles, one that smelt like vanilla, the other unscented. After selecting two glass holders for them, they strolled back towards his LoDo loft.

At home, she placed one on the table and the other on the vanity of the master bathroom.

"They make your place feel more lived in," she said, returning to him.

He was in the kitchen slicing a lime for the glasses of sparkling mineral water that he'd just poured. His loft was as sparse as hers was cluttered. He hadn't noticed how sterile his was until now.

Niles laid down the knife on the cutting board.

"Oh, oh, Sir." She clutched her hands in front of her.

"What?" he asked.

"You have that look."

"What look?"

"The one where you're going to ravish me."

"If I hadn't been planning that before, I am now." He pulled her against him. "Open your mouth," he said. "I've wanted to taste you all afternoon." He sought out her tongue. At first he was as easy-going as he had been on the dance floor last night. But always, where she was concerned, carnality unfurled inside him.

She responded in kind, reaching around him, moaning, granting him deeper access.

All of a sudden, it was about far more than the kiss. It was about them, about how she reacted to him.

He was with subs all the time, and this interaction was beyond that. Though she never overstepped his unspoken boundaries, she pushed him in ways no one else did. He liked that about her, even as it frustrated him. She tasted of sunshine and laughter, but that was undercut by the danger she presented. This supple submissive made him question everything he'd promised himself. The idea he wanted her around for more than just a day conflicted with his sworn promise to never fall in love again. Still, the way she felt in his arms left him thinking about tomorrow. "Damn," he said as he ended the kiss. "We should make out more often."

"Is that what that was?" she asked from the protective sphere of his arms.

"Having sex with clothes on?"

"That's what it felt like to me." He left her long enough to lower the blinds. "I love your breasts."

"They're for you, Sir."

"Damn fucking right," he said. "Now get that shirt off."

She took hold of the hem and tugged the material up over her head and dropped it on the floor. The bra quickly followed as did her panties, jeans and platform sandals. Then she was standing in front of him in her necklace and nothing else. It looked beautiful against her creamy skin.

"Crawl to the guest room," he ordered. "First door on the right. I want to watch your ass."

"My pleasure, Sir."

The little vixen took her time lowering herself to the floor, and he couldn't look away. With an exaggerated sway of her hips, she preceded him down the hall. He followed, captivated, seduced, wondering who was the one being mastered.

Though he had never scened in his home, this week he'd bought a few things with the intention of hosting her.

Because he knew she'd like it, he'd installed a hook in the ceiling and purchased a thuddy flogger. "I want to secure you by your hair," he told her.

"Yes, please," she said from her place on her knees.

While she was totally different than Eleanor had been, he loved her responses. She hadn't become a sub because it was something he wanted. She'd been one when they met. "I love that you embrace your submissiveness."

"Not everyone has appreciated that, Sir. Thank you."

He gathered her hair and placed a band at the top to make a ponytail. Niles placed an additional band midway down and a final one at the bottom to keep it secure. Though he'd done this several times for video, there was nothing perfunctory about his motions. In fact, it seemed deeply meaningful to him. Her deep, steady breaths added to the atmosphere. "Stand please."

Keeping her eyes downcast, she did so.

"Raise your arms." He cuffed her hands to his overhead hook.

Her breaths became farther apart as she turned herself over to his ministrations and settled in with trust.

He secured her hair to the cuffs with a hemp rope and a square knot.

She made a soft sound of approval.

"You like this," he observed.

"I do, Sir."

He was aware that her body was getting warmer. Niles forced himself to focus, something that wasn't usually an issue for him. He treated each scene like the job it had become. And now, he was remembering how reverent the act was when two people had a relationship outside of the dominance. "I told you previously your breasts need to be marked."

"I love having them whipped, Sir. By you."

"Legs farther apart, sub."

She followed his instruction and that changed her stance, putting more weight on her hair and wrists, pulling her head back. It exposed her neck more and made it less likely he'd catch her face with a strand.

Niles opened a drawer and pulled out a flogger. He held it up in front of her, and she kissed the handle.

With slow, gentle blows, he smacked her with the leather. As she closed her eyes and began to moan, he struck harder, no longer moving over her torso but concentrating on her breasts.

"Mark them, Sir," she pleaded.

He changed the tempo, hitting harder and harder.

"Thank you," she murmured.

Taking a break, Niles fingered her wet pussy. It amazed him how quickly she responded to him. She began to jerk against him, and he gave her nipples a vicious twist.

"W-want to come, Sir."

"Wait." Seeing her desperate attempt to squeeze her thighs together for some relief, he snapped, "Keep those legs apart."

In her bondage, Brandy sagged even farther forward.

"That's a gorgeous sub."

Timing was a crucial part of each scene.

He started over, working until he had her moaning. He slapped her pussy with the leather thongs and her movements pulled on her hair.

"This is wonderful, Sir."

She didn't endure, she enjoyed.

Now that her body was warm, glowing, relaxed, he beat her breasts in earnest, stinging with the leather tips and with the impact of the broadside of the strands.

"My nipples....more."

"Whatever you want." This was trickier, and he adjusted his position for precision. He beat her nipples and her breasts, varying the location, speed and amount of pain he delivered.

Her cries became whimpers then moans then something so much more...surrendered bliss.

He released his knot and cuffs, seemingly without her noticing. She hadn't moved her legs or tried to sneak an orgasm. Instead, she'd given herself to him without question. Telling her how pleased he was with her, he rubbed her arms to restore circulation then pulled out the bands that held her hair. He finger-combed it, but the strands remained kinked. An outward, but private sign of her submission.

"If it pleases you, Sir, I'd love to fuck."

He drew her towards the master bedroom, and he paused in front of a full-length mirror. Their gazes met and locked in the reflection and he traced one of the marks that temporarily marred her breast.

"Thank you, again."

He pulled back the bedspread and turned down the sheets before picking her up and putting her on the bed. He kissed the welts before licking her pussy.

"Sir, I hope this isn't a continuation of your torture," she said.

"You can come," he said. He manipulated her clit with his finger and fucked her with his tongue.

"Never felt anything like it, Sir," she said, digging her heels in and pressing her pussy into his face.

He moved faster and faster, meeting her incessant demands.

"Master Niles," she whispered.

He spanked her pussy hard, and she jerked as she climaxed, leaving her taste on his tongue.

For a few minutes, he held her, luxuriating in the feel of her hair as it spilled over his body.

"I'd do that again," she said.

"Which part?"

"All of it." She turned on her side. "But I was talking about the hair part. It's just so damn animalistic."

"Animalistic?"

"Like this..." She straddled him and tugged his T-shirt from his jeans.

Eleanor would have never been so bold. At the Den, neither would Brandy. But here, her natural personality shone. He liked it—her—more and more.

For a man who had spent the better part of a few years as a recluse, he was adjusting to having a woman around with alarming ease.

She managed to pull off his T-shirt, and she threw it on the floor.

While he removed his pants, something that couldn't happen quickly enough, she grabbed a condom from the drawer he indicated, and she rolled it down his cock using her mouth and no hands. By the time it was secure, he was ready to come.

Then she climbed on top of him.

"May I?" she asked.

"Beg."

"Oh, Master Niles, please...I want your cock."

She slid her pussy over his cock. If she kept it up, he'd be the one begging.

"I need to have your big cock in my pussy or I will shrivel up and die."

He laughed. "That's a bit excessive, don't you think?"

"You have no idea what it feels like to be me," she said.

There was honesty layered beneath her teasing tone, and it rocked him.

"Please?"

He took her by the hips, lifted her and seated her on his dick. She took him, sighing as he filled her tight pussy. "Ride me, gorgeous sub."

Digging her knees into the mattress, she did, raising herself so that only his cockhead was at her entrance, then sinking low.

At first, she took her time, long and slow.

Then, he felt her pussy tighten. Her movements were quick and short, and he lifted her up. "Give me your climax."

She pitched forward, changing the angle of his penetration so he was pressing against her G-spot.

Brandy trembled. Then with a gasp, she shuddered, squeezing his cock hard.

When her climax ebbed, she collapsed on his chest, and he enveloped her. Her hair shrouded them, and her body was slick with perspiration.

"I've never known a woman who seemed to enjoy sex as much as you do," he said.

"It's never been like it is with you, Sir."

He moved his hands lower and adjusted her body so he could bury himself inside her up to his balls.

Keeping his hands on her hips, he jack-knifed his hips, surging in her.

"You're going to make me come again, Sir," she managed breathlessly.

She placed a hand on one of his shoulders for balance as he rose a final time.

Lost in her, he pulled her down and trapped her against him. "Damn," he said, shooting his load.

It wasn't just her. He'd never been so hungry for a woman before. For years, he'd gone without regular sex, and until now, he hadn't missed it. With Brandy, the more he was with her, the more he wanted.

As he inhaled the fresh scent of peaches that lingered on her hair and felt the flutter of her pulse, he knew one thing for certain. He didn't want to share her.

He routinely spent time shooting videos. A compelling, sex-infused illusion was created for the viewer, but there was rarely a connection between any of the participants. Many were friends off set and often went for a drink or food afterwards. But they were all professionals. They showed up to work, not have an illicit affair.

So he knew the same was true for Brandy. She enjoyed submission, liked the money, had responsibilities to take care of.

But he wanted to be the only man fucking her. The idea of watching other men force her to kneel, chain her to a wall, lick her cunt or whip her ripe breasts made fire churn in his belly. He didn't have the right to ask her to quit, and he was a selfish bastard for even entertaining the thought. But there it was.

He disposed of the condom then came back to tuck her into bed. She was already on her side, curled up, so he snuggled in behind her, holding her possessively close.

* * * *

When he awakened on Sunday morning, she was outside on the balcony, a cup of coffee sitting beside her on a small metal table. She had pulled her bare feet up onto the chair and was using her knees as a table of sorts for a pad of paper.

From inside, he watched her. Her hand moved quickly across the page. Engrossed, she never paused or looked up.

She'd dressed in jeans and the T-shirt he'd discarded last night. He found her every bit as enticing as when she was naked.

He returned to the kitchen and poured himself a cup of the coffee. With the first sip, he decided this would be her chore in the future. He wasn't sure what she did differently, but this tasted richer, more complex.

After pulling on a pair of jeans, he watched her again, waiting until she took a break.

Carrying his coffee, he walked onto the patio.

She looked up and smiled.

The temperature seemed to increase ten degrees.

She put down the pad and pen then rose onto her toes to kiss his cheek. "I hope you don't mind that I raided your home office for supplies."

"You keep making the coffee and anything I have is yours."

"Yours really is dreadful," she said. "Oh, wait. Did I say that out loud?"

He put down his cup and smacked her bottom, the sound more impressive because his hand had landed on denim.

She yelped, but grinned. "Again, Sir, that's no incentive to make me behave."

"It wasn't meant to," he said. His voice emerged gruffer than he'd intended.

"Then we're thinking along the same lines," she said, rising on her toes again to loop her hands around his neck. "I know I'm being presumptuous, Sir, but will you kiss me?"

He did. Long and slow. When he ended it, they were both breathless. Her nipples were erect and pressing against him.

His hard-on was from more than morning interest, it was a deep-seated desire for one woman. Before sitting, he adjusted his pants.

With her gaze, she tracked all of his movements.

"What are you working on?" he asked, picking up his cup.

She handed over her pad. "Ideas for your website. And I didn't like anything I did with your logo, so I took another swipe at it."

He nodded. "Even freehand, this is good. Cleaned up on the computer, it will be crisp and sharp."

"I'll try to get you something by tomorrow. If you're interested, you can flip back a couple of pages and find some ideas for your aunt's rebranding. More blues and greens."

"Less pink?"

"I didn't say that."

"You didn't have to."

"I've updated the font and kept most of the information, just broken up instead of long paragraphs."

"May I?"

"Please." She handed over a pen.

He added a few arrows to move stuff around then handed back the pad.

"Could work." She nodded. "I like it. Any ideas on yours?"

He flipped to a blank piece of paper. He sketched in his logo then placed his company name below it and to the right. He added a bold line next to it.

"Might work."

"You sound sceptical."

"You're the client." She smiled. "I'm happy to do whatever you want."

"That means you don't like it."

"I wouldn't say that," she returned.

"Then...?"

"It sucks."

He winced. "You don't hold back."

"Would you prefer that I keep my opinion to myself?"

"Point taken."

Together, they took turns with the notepad until they both nodded.

"I'll mock it up on the computer and get it back to you in the next day or two."

"We make a good team."

Laughing, they clinked the rims of their cups together. She took a drink and wrinkled her nose.

"It's cold."

"Yeah. Mine, too."

By unspoken agreement, they went inside. She dumped out the old coffee and he refilled the cups. Then he made breakfast.

The sun had burst through some early-morning clouds, and they ate their food al fresco.

Afterwards, they cleaned the kitchen. He loaded the dishwasher while she put items away and wiped down the granite countertops.

For a moment, he studied her, imagining them having breakfast together every day. The thought of a future caught him off guard. He tried to shove it away, but it remained persistent. "Shall I brew another pot of coffee?" he asked to fill the booming silence.

She shook her head. He noticed that her hair still had waves from last night's bondage. Until she tamed it, it would be a reminder of their time together, every bit as much as the couple of still-fading welts she was sure to have.

"No?"

"I need to be going. I'll stop in Frisco and grab one."

"You don't have to leave," he said.

"Reality calls. I need to be at the Den at four," she said. "And the menagerie will need some attention. I have a couple of project deadlines this week. And I didn't get through as much laundry as I'd hoped before I left Granby last week." Keeping distance between them, she added, "Thank you, Sir. I had a wonderful weekend. I've never been spoilt like that before."

"You deserve it, Brandy, and so much more."

"Like I said, reality intrudes."

There was so much more he wanted to say. But words failed him. Instead, he put on shoes while she slipped into her sandals and gathered her toiletries from the counter in the master bathroom.

Outside, he put her luggage in the car trunk before opening the driver's door for her.

As she slid behind the wheel, she gave him a fragile smile.

"Let me know when you get home," he said.

"I've got a ton of things to accomplish before I go to work," she hedged.

He scowled. "I'd appreciate a telephone call to let me know you're safe."

"I've made that drive dozens of times. I'll be fine. I will send you an email when I have something to show you, though."

Her fake sunny smile pissed him off. "Is there a reason you're refusing to call?"

"Of course," she said.

"Of course?" he repeated, shoving his hands in his pockets. If she'd grabbed a battering ram and knocked him in the head, he couldn't have been caught more unprepared by her answer. He'd expected her capitulation or, at worst, for her to demure politely. "Enlighten me."

"We had a great weekend, and I appreciate your hospitality. But let's not fool ourselves into thinking that it's anything more." She slid into the driver's seat and stabbed the key into the ignition.

"Friends would let each other know they're okay."

"Not always."

"What the hell happened back there, Brandy?"

"Nothing."

"That's a lie. I demand better than that. I deserve better than that."

She laid her forehead on the steering wheel before pushing away and looking at him. "Sir..." She sighed. "Master Niles. Can I be truthful? You know about my relationship with Reyes. What you don't know is I have to protect myself from my own brand of craziness. You once asked if I collected animals instead of humans. I do. I'd be an idiot to spend any more time with you, not because I don't like you but because I could really like you. I adore your crazy aunt. I like the sex. The way I feel when I'm with you is amazing. Please. *Please*, let me go."

He should honour her wishes, but he couldn't. He put his body in the way of the car door closing. "Can we talk about this?"

"No. I've said what I needed to. I've been as honest as I can be."

"Does it have to be all or nothing?"

"For me. Yes. It does."

Her voice sounded rough from the emotion she fought back. Niles had wandered into a field of emotional landmines, and he had no fucking sense of how to navigate the terrain. He knew she'd breathed joy into his life and he didn't want to let her go. "I'd like to see you again."

"That's not a good idea."

"What the hell do you mean by that?"

Her body sagged a little. "We live too far apart." She took a breath and met his gaze. "And I'm talking about far more than miles."

Part of him didn't want to release her, but he'd never hold a woman against her will. "Brandy…"

She reached for the door handle.

Having no other choice, he stepped away while she sealed herself off from him. She backed out and took off, all without ever looking back.

Chapter Eight

Life sucked.

It didn't matter how Brandy looked at it, in the last month she'd never been more bored and restless, as well as lonely.

As she turned over her car to the Den's valet, she automatically scanned the parking area for Master Niles' luxury SUV. She exhaled in relief when she didn't see it.

Brandy reminded herself it was early. There were only a handful of vehicles in sight, and they belonged to staff members. It had become a habit to look, though, each time she arrived. If she was going to run into him, she wanted to be prepared.

Dozens of times over the last month, she'd told herself that walking away from Master Niles had been the prudent—and only—choice. On the drive home, she'd taken off the necklace he'd given her and dropped it in her purse.

That morning on his patio, when he'd taken her notepad and added his ideas to hers, creating something unique, she'd realised he was beginning to matter to her. She'd liked the blending of their thoughts. It had energised her, made her feel vibrant.

After breakfast, she'd carried their dishes back into the kitchen. As always, she'd been amazed by how natural hanging out together seemed to be.

When she'd wiped down the counter, she'd caught him looking at her. She'd read the desire in his eyes. The haunted expression that had defined him over the years had vanished. He was no longer the Dom who'd been sitting outside at the Den's private party, looking so formidable that she'd debated whether or not to approach him.

Now, not for the first time, she wished she hadn't.

During the time at her home and at his, she had seen how deep he was, laughed with him, met his aunt, learnt about his businesses, been cared for by him. And damn it, he'd even sent a rubber foot to her nasty little wiener dog.

As much as she hated to admit it, in retrospect, Gregorio had been right. Master Niles was a man she should have never become involved with.

She'd been accurate when she'd told him there were too many miles between them, literal and figurative. She had a humble, unassuming life in a small mountain town. He had his fingers in five or six different businesses and a lifestyle to match.

From the beginning, he'd been clear that he didn't intend to get involved in another relationship again.

One of them had needed to be smart.

If she'd continued, she might have ended up losing herself again. With him, so powerful and commanding, it would be all-too easy.

The ghosts may have been vanquished from his eyes, but she was afraid they'd moved to her heart.

He wasn't making it easy for her to keep her distance, though. He'd approved her website design. Every few days, he sent a polite request for an update. Like the coward she was, she'd moved his project to one side while she worked on other things, like his aunt's marketing campaign.

A week after the silent auction, he'd sent her the Denver Nuggets tickets she'd been so excited about. Of course, they were courtside, close enough to see the players sweat. And they were for the upcoming home opener against one of the greatest rivals in franchise history.

He'd included a note telling her he'd love to go, but that she was free to invite someone else. They were her gift, and she could do whatever she wanted with them, as long as she enjoyed the evening. Margot would probably be the happy recipient of the extra ticket, much to John's disappointment, but guilt told her he should be in the seat next to her.

She entered the Den and saw Gregorio in the kitchen. Giving him a half-hearted wave, she went straight to the ladies' locker room. Since her time with Master Niles, she'd managed to avoid private conversation with Gregorio, and she wanted to keep it that way.

She changed into a short skirt, spiky heels and an interesting, sheer shirt that had only one sleeve, leaving the opposite shoulder and arm bare.

With a flick of her wrist, Brandy slammed her locker door shut, ready for another now-meaningless evening at the Den. She hadn't lost the joy of submission, she'd just lost the enthusiasm for giving it to any different number of men each weekend. She wanted to be on her knees for one particular Dom.

And since he had no interest in being that man, she'd been smart to escape when she did.

"We need to talk."

Brandy looked up to see Gregorio standing inside the doorway.

"This is the ladies' room," she informed him.

When he spread his legs, folded his arms across his chest and raised his eyebrows, she sighed. Tonight he looked even more rugged than usual. He wore masculine motorcycle boots, a pair of painted-on pants and a leather vest that hung open over his smooth, olive-coloured skin. Doms and subs alike would like to get their hands on this bad boy switch.

"I've known you, what, five years? It's not like you to be lethargic."

"My freelance business has taken off." It was close enough to the truth that he should believe her. "Once I meet a couple of deadlines, I'll be fine."

"Other people might accept that. I don't."

When she tipped her chin and swallowed the stupid lump that had unexpectedly lodged in her throat, he took a step towards her.

"Master Niles?"

"No."

"He looked like shit the other night."

Her pulse hammered. "When did you see him?"

"His production company had a shoot up here."

She sank onto the bench behind her. Brandy had purposefully shoved aside flashes of images of him dominating other women — sexy, beautiful models and actresses. Even though she suspected he wouldn't get involved with any of them, it was always a possibility, and the idea tortured her.

"So this *is* about him," Gregorio guessed.

"You were right. Is that what you wanted to hear? I shouldn't have seen him."

"Oh, honey. You've got the biggest heart of anyone I know."

"Dumb, aren't I?"

He shook his head. "It was inevitable."

"He's pretty cool."

"Broken."

Gregorio hadn't seen the grooves ease from beside Master Niles' eyes.

"I never wanted to be right," Gregorio said.

"Next time I'll listen to you." She went into his arms and gathered strength for at least a minute.

"For the record? He hired someone else to emcee the scene. He didn't participate in the video. Told Master Damien he was going to be stepping back to pursue other interests after he gets some people trained, said part of it depends on his redesigned website going live."

She stepped away from Gregorio. His news stunned her.

Master Niles was no longer working in his own company, and he'd sent a veiled message to her through Gregorio.

"Let us know if you'd like us to fire you or whether you'd prefer to turn in your notice."

"I... What?" She stared at him, trying to comprehend what he'd said, but unable to make sense of the words.

"We've had no complaints. But you can't tell me your heart is in this."

"You're *firing* me?"

"Do you really want to stay?"

"This is unexpected."

"Is it? Or have you been moving towards it all along?"

"This is part of who I am, my social life, my friends. It gives me something to do so that the weekends aren't unbearably long." She sighed. "You can't fire me."

He laughed from somewhere deep inside. "I'm afraid I can. You can tell me I was right later."

"Fuck you," she said.

"Honey, go home. Think about it."

"You're really terminating me?"

"In that capacity."

"What other capacity is there?" she asked, not even trying to be polite. She was too flummoxed, overwhelmed.

"We've had complaints about the newsletter not being timely enough, about links not working, about members not being able to find information on special events."

Her mouth fell open. "Are you offering me a new job?"

"Honey, you're a part of the Den. We wouldn't be able to let you go entirely."

"I don't know what to say." Never in her entire life had she been given a pink slip and a job opportunity in the space of three minutes.

"Think of it as a transfer from one department to another."

"I'd be working here?"

"From home."

She felt adrift.

In a hazy state, she cleaned out her locker, dumping the contents into her bag.

Gregorio made no move to help or to leave the room. When she had everything, she flicked the locker door, sending it flying, and hearing it slam with a horrible, harsh, satisfying slap of metal on metal. "Bill me for damages."

Bag slung over her shoulder, she walked back towards the front door. Gregorio followed, and it occurred to her she was being escorted out. Her pay cheque and purple wrist band lay on the check-in table.

"I'll buy you dinner tomorrow."

"No, thanks," she replied. "I'll be all right."

"Brandy—"

"Give me some time, okay?"

He held up his hands. "You have my phone number."

What the hell was she supposed to do now?

Her car was still outside where she'd left it. She did the only thing she could think of. She texted Margot to open a bottle of wine.

When she arrived at their home, John was in his man cave, and Margot had already poured them each a glass.

Like a good friend, Margot offered Brandy a job waiting tables. "But you'd have to wear a few more clothes than you did at the Den."

"No she doesn't!" John called from the other room.

"Turn up the sound on the damned television!" Margot called back.

Brandy giggled at the idea of wearing something outrageously short to work at the diner. Then she remembered the kilt that Master Niles had been excited about. She hiccoughed and her eyes filled with tears.

"You upset her!" Margot yelled to John.

"No he didn't. I upset me."

"Okay, explain."

"I can't."

"Even better. Drink up."

After making arrangements for the pets to be taken care of, Brandy spent the night on her friends' couch and stayed there even when they left the house at four o'clock to open the restaurant.

When Brandy awakened at nine, the house was quiet, and she felt surprisingly good and more than a bit guilty at having slept while Margot and John had gone to work. Margot had stayed up late and listened to the story of Brandy's woes when it came to Master Niles. And she'd heard all about Brandy's fabulous necklace. Twice.

Brandy tidied up the living room and washed the wine glasses before driving home.

She'd spent the last two years working a tight schedule, juggling the Den while building her other business. And now the absence of a defined schedule left her aimless. Waiting tables would give her purpose and force her to get out of bed, but the idea of getting up at the same time she often went to bed made her cringe.

Later that day, restless after walking the dogs and getting food for the lizards, she returned to work on her business. Master Damien had sent an email outlining the things he'd like to see in a proposal from her.

He'd signed the email in a cordial way and said how much he was looking forward to seeing her soon. "Not likely," she muttered.

MW jumped up and ran over, as if Brandy had spoken to him.

She moved Master Damien's email to a projects folder so she didn't have to look at it. She was still miffed, and he could wait a day or so for an answer.

But avoiding Master Damien's email provided all the motivation she needed to pull up a draft of Master Niles' new website.

Since she no longer had to keep to a specific schedule, she stayed up all night and sent him a beta version of it on Thursday afternoon. And of course, she checked her email every five minutes to see if he'd replied.

When he didn't get back to her right away, her imagination supplied a dozen different reasons why. Maybe he'd grown tired of waiting and hired someone else. Maybe he'd taken one of the willing subs to Belize with him. "Stop," she told herself, getting up and pacing the floor.

Gregorio had told her Master Niles wasn't shooting videos at the Den anymore.

Which, now that she thought about it, also meant he'd found someone else and gone to Belize.

For the first time since she'd walked away, she wondered what would have happened if she hadn't left. What if she'd stayed and talked, like he wanted? What if she'd agreed when he'd said he wanted to see her again?

Her reasons for leaving were still legitimate. The two hour drive between their places was daunting enough. Having animals in his urban setting wouldn't work. And she didn't see such an imposing man living in her house.

She'd run in order to avoid getting her heart broken. The joke was on her. Even though they'd spent such a short time together, she'd fallen in love with him. It was hard to imagine she could be any more devastated than she was right then.

* * * *

In Brandy's driveway, Niles turned off his car engine.

Enough was enough.

Showing up here uninvited was risky, no doubt. At one time, he'd lived on the leading edge. He'd started businesses, invested in uncertain ventures, failed a number of times, lost buckets of money then tried again. He'd given his heart to Eleanor and been crushed when he'd lost her. He had no idea how he'd endured the first few months. When he looked back, he had no recollection of the endless blur of days.

But it wasn't like him to get stuck in a morass of pain, nor would Eleanor have expected it of him. She had urged him to live fully as a celebration of what they'd shared.

It had taken half a year for him to return to work, and even then, he hadn't gone back fulltime.

Brandy, with her persistent questions and the way she'd brought candles into his loft, had prised apart the heart he'd thought he'd sealed shut.

He hadn't wanted her to leave when she had. But as he'd watched her drive away, he'd told himself she was right. He'd been frank about his decision not to enter another permanent relationship. And her experiences with Reyes would give any woman cause for concern, especially a submissive with a heart as big as hers.

She needed a Dom strong enough to step up, give her freedom to be who she wanted to be, and a man strong enough to care for her in return.

It hadn't taken him three days to figure out he appreciated the energy she brought into his life. He'd sent her the basketball tickets. When she hadn't responded, he'd repeatedly asked about the website.

He'd run out of patience, a virtue he'd always thought was overrated.

Before he knocked, he heard MW's high-pitched yips and Dana's howls. Whisper meandered over and wound around his legs.

Brandy opened the door and leaned against the jamb.

He saw the breath go out of her.

"Master Niles."

"I had a few things to go over about the website."

"You could have emailed," she said, raking her hair back from her forehead.

"I could have."

"Or called."

"True."

"Or sent a text message."

"Also accurate." Jesus, she looked good. Obviously she hadn't been expecting company. She had on fuzzy pink slippers and faded-to-white jeans with a hole in one knee. Her grey sweatshirt was at least two sizes too big and did nothing to diminish his desire.

"Maybe smoke signals."

"My fire-starting skills are a bit rusty."

"And I've got the flamethrower." Finally, she smiled.

"Can I come in?"

She stepped aside, pulling the dogs back in with her. He closed the door and caught sight of the necklace he'd given her, sitting atop of a stack of yellow legal pads on the kitchen table. "I figured it would be in a jewellery box."

"I like looking at it," she admitted.

Parts of the silver were marred by her fingerprints. "Looks better on you," he said.

MW dragged over his rubber foot. Demanding to be petted, Dana nudged Niles' hand. Whisper hadn't followed him in. But with that 'fingernails on chalkboard' sound, he came in through the pet door.

"Why are you here?" she asked, leaning against the counter, keeping the distance of half a room between them.

"For you," he said plainly. "I let you go. It was foolish."

"You didn't let me go. I walked away."

"Because you were scared."

She shrugged. "And? Nothing has changed, except you drove for two hours because you were too stubborn to listen to me before."

"Something has changed."

"What's that, Sir?"

"Me."

"I'm not sure I understand."

"I want you in my life. A woman. A sub. A wife."

"A…" Her jaw fell open.

Dana trotted over to Brandy and sat by her side.

"What? Why?"

"I didn't think I could fall in love again, but I did. I don't want to live without you. You don't have to give up yourself. If I fail, I think you're annoyingly persistent enough to keep at me."

"Me?" she asked with an air of innocence.

"I love you, Brandy Hess."

"Oh, Sir… I don't know what to say."

"Yes will suffice. Yes, Sir, would be even better."

In response, she crossed the room and knelt before him. Time froze then fractured into a million possibilities. "Tell me," he urged.

MW nipping at her toes interrupted the moment. He suspected that would happen far more often in the future than he would like. Still, it was for his sub. Niles picked up the rubber foot and tossed it into the living room. Distracted, MW raced after it. "You were saying, sub?"

"I love you, Master Niles." She met his gaze. Her eyes blue as a cloudless sky radiated the heat of her inner beauty. "Yes. Yes, yes, Sir."

He pulled her to her feet and against him, kissing her deeply. "How much time do we have?"

"Sir?"

"Before you have to go to the Den?"

"I figured you had heard. I don't work there anymore. They realised my heart wasn't in it and let me go."

"You were fired?"

"I'm not sorry," she said.

He dug his hand in her hair and used it as leverage to tip back her head. "I'm not sorry that I don't have to share you," he admitted.

"What about my menagerie?" she asked. "And I will need to take in more dogs on a foster basis from time to time."

"We'll work it out. I'll move up here, or we'll get a bigger place in town. I'd never ask you to get rid of the pests. I mean pets."

She smiled.

"At least for now, I'd like you to wear that particular necklace. The circle represents a collar, but it's on a larger chain, and that represents the way we're tied together."

"I'd be honoured, Sir. I love it." She lifted her hair and he put it on her.

She breathed out. For a second, she closed her eyes. "Thank you, my Master."

"Thank you, gorgeous sub."

She fingered the circle. "I really do like it."

Repeating what he'd mentioned at the hotel, "It has whatever meaning you give it."

"Then it means my heart belongs to you."

His cock lengthened. This woman, every moment with her, was worth any risk. "You can help me choose your wedding ring."

"You can help me choose, Sir," she corrected. "I'm the one who will have to wear it all day every day for the rest of my life."

"Annoyingly persistent," he said with a long-suffering sigh.

"Part of my charm."

"I think you need to be put in your place, sub."

"Indeed, Sir."

"Your bedroom," he instructed.

"Mind if I change, and you can join me in a few minutes?"

"Make it worth the wait."

When she called his name, he entered the bedroom and let out a deep, appreciative wolf-whistle. His sub was dressed in a white button-down shirt, exposing her cleavage. The necklace nestled there. Five inch heels lengthened her calves. The showstopper was the stupid-short kilt that had fuelled his fantasies for more than thirty nights. "It's even better in reality," he said, voice suddenly hoarse. "Is it true that people wear nothing beneath a kilt?"

"Shall I show you, Sir?"

"Yeah." The word was guttural, he wondered if she'd understood him. "Bend over and touch your toes." He took a couple of steps towards her.

Her movements sassy and seductive, she did. The tartan rode up, exposing her rounded cheeks, and, God help him, a stainless steel butt plug with silver crystals refracting light a hundred directions. "Unbelievable." No sub had ever surprised him, delighted him this much.

He stripped then took out a condom from her nightstand drawer.

"I'm ready for you, Sir."

He fingered between her labia and found her moist. "You are."

"The very thought of you fucking me arouses me, Sir."

"With the plug, this will be tight," he warned.

"The way I wanted it, Sir."

Reverently he parted her buttocks, leaving her off-balance, depending on him to keep her stable. He held her hips to keep her secure.

Even with her heels, he had to bend his knees to enter her pussy.

He gritted his teeth to keep from spilling prematurely. The sharpness of her scent, the wetness of her pussy and the tightness because of the plug stuffed up her ass were a near-lethal combination.

"I want all of you, Sir."

Goaded by her honesty, he took her with a single thrust.

She screamed, and he caught her weight as she pitched forward.

"I've needed this," she said, her voice hardly audible.

"Me, too," he responded. He fucked her hard, then pulled out before he ejaculated.

"Sir?"

He helped her to stand and look at him. "I want to finish this differently." Niles placed her on the bed, then entered her with slow strokes, watching her expression.

She kept her eyes open, meeting his gaze. Even if she hadn't told him she loved him, he'd have known by looking in the crystalline depths.

Brandy wrapped her arms around his neck.

"Who am I?"

"My Master," she answered. "My love. My husband-to-be."

All three sounded right. Perfect.

He fucked her hard, claiming her. He made sure she came, crying out his name.

Then he sought his own release, sealing their mutual promise. "Mine," he said.

"Yours," she agreed, cradling his face. "Yours, Sir. Now. Always. *Yours.*"

MASTERED

Sierra Cartwright

A secret part of her
is intrigued...

IN THE
DEN

Mastered: In the Den

Sierra Cartwright

Released February 2014

Excerpt

Chapter One

Damien Lowell always got what he wanted. Granted, sometimes the challenge was greater than he anticipated. But that didn't matter. The more difficult the task, the more he relished it. Working hard for something flexed his mental muscles, sharpened his senses and fed his creative energy.

Right now he was standing with his arms folded across his chest, his focus on the gorgeous dark-haired Domme on the other side of the room.

Tonight she'd used kohl liner and several layers of mascara to add drama and depth to her startling green eyes. Her hair hung over her shoulders and cascaded down her back in a shining mahogany waterfall.

She wore thigh-high black boots with heels so tall he was amazed she could walk in them. Fishnet stockings were attached to a garter belt, and her tiny black skirt barely covered her buttocks. She'd topped the breathtaking outfit with a leather corset that he itched to unlace.

As if sensing his perusal, she glanced over and raised her glass in salute. He inclined his head in acknowledgment.

As she sipped, she continued to regard him.

This was a bit of an unusual circumstance for him at the Den. He'd bought the massive mountain estate years before, and he'd turned it into a private and exclusive BDSM club. While female dominants were welcomed and accorded the respect due their position, less than two dozen had applied for membership.

Most of the women he associated with here were subs. They didn't meet and hold his gaze like Mistress Catrina.

After several seconds, she severed the contact and returned her attention to her submissive. She snagged a canapé from a passing server and offered it to the bare chested man kneeling before her. Since he sported spikey blond hair, the pair presented a striking contrast.

The man, on a leash and wearing nothing other than tight, gold-coloured shorts, looked up at her adoringly as he opened his mouth. She smiled and brushed a hand across his forehead. She drew him in closer, then popped the treat into his mouth.

All the while, Damien pictured the Domme on her knees, affixed to *his* leash, fully understanding what it meant to submit.

He'd known her for several years and he knew she was an excellent mistress. Recently she'd attended a private event he'd hosted. That evening, he'd witnessed a deeper, more contemplative side of her. At one point, she'd stood in front of a window, gazing into the distance. When he'd joined her, she'd faced him. For a moment, before she'd schooled it away, he'd seen a groove between her sculptured eyebrows. When he'd asked how she was enjoying the evening, she'd responded with politeness. But she'd excused herself and left soon after.

Damien didn't often allow his thoughts to be consumed by women, especially dominant ones. But since that night, he hadn't been able to get thoughts of Mistress Catrina out of his mind.

"How's it going, Boss?"

Damien turned his attention to the Den's second-in-command, Gregorio. Hiring the man had been one of the smartest strategic decisions Damien had ever made. Gregorio lived onsite in a caretaker cottage. He ensured the safety of their guests, and he oversaw the estate when it was open for a production company's use. Not only that, but he managed the calendar, the employees, the accounting and maintenance. As if that were not enough, he also participated in scenes. Since he could top or bottom, he was even more valuable to the house.

Gregorio folded his arms across his chest. Tonight he had on a black T-shirt beneath a leather vest. With his silver earring and motorcycle boots, he looked suitably intimidating. "Your demonstration starts in fifteen minutes, Boss." He hooked a thumb and pointed over his shoulder. "Good turnout."

They'd had plenty of reservations for the annual open house extravaganza. "There are a lot of new faces," Damien agreed.

"And buttocks," Gregorio added with a grin.

Despite a widespread snowstorm, guests had arrived from all over the region, including parts of Wyoming, Kansas, even Montana. Gregorio had planned ahead, reserving a block of hotel rooms in the nearby ski town of Winter Park. Skilled staff shuttled people back and forth in four-wheel drive vehicles.

"Sarah went to the ladies' locker room to prepare. She'll meet you in the entranceway. Your items are laid out on the mantel as requested."

Damien nodded. "Great job, as always."

"All in a day's work," Gregorio said. "I'll be assisting you onstage." With a nod, he excused himself.

Mistress Catrina was no longer in sight, and Damien wondered if she'd taken her submissive downstairs to one of the private rooms.

Demonstrations typically drew a number of neophytes and people curious about joining the club. During that time, long-time members often took advantage of the uncrowded conditions in the dungeon to connect and scene.

He went upstairs to his private suite and flicked on the fireplace to banish the winter chill. The blinds were open, and snow drifted past the massive windows. Another stunning Colorado night, cold and windy, perfect for sleep — or other things — in the custom-built bed.

In the backyard area, the fire pit blazed and a few well-dressed hearty souls stood around it.

After changing into black leather pants and a short-sleeved T-shirt, he clipped a whip to his side and went back down the stairs in time to see Mistress Catrina placing her empty champagne flute on a passing waiter's tray. So, she was still in the public area. He tried not to show how ridiculously pleased he was. "Catrina," he said by way of greeting.

"Damien," she returned, glancing at him through long, enhanced lashes.

He wondered what she looked like natural, naked, on her knees, her lips trembling as she waited for him. Then he shoved the thought away. No sense allowing his imagination free rein. He'd enjoyed success in business because he was pragmatic, not fanciful. "Enjoying the evening?" he asked.

"Of course."

"I'll take that as a polite lie."

She scowled. "Your events are always fabulous."

"So why aren't you having a good time?"

"You're the one who said I'm not," she countered.

Her scent was as exotic as she was. Musk and vanilla, layered with a pervasive sexual need. He wondered if he was the only one who'd noticed it. "Where's your boy?"

"He's outside having a smoke. Bad habit," she said. "But who am I to judge?" She shrugged, her creamy shoulders rising and falling before settling into a gentle slope.

"Who, indeed?"

"We only hooked up for part of the evening."

"That collar isn't yours?"

"No. I've never formally collared anyone. That particular one belongs to Master Lawrence. We're hoping he makes it up here tonight." She shrugged. "But with the weather..."

A sudden urge to wrap his fingers around her upper arms and drag her to her toes assailed him. But that would violate personal as well as house rules. He owed her the same respect accorded to all dominants. In all his years of being a Dom, he'd never had the urge to drive a Domme to her knees. Until now. "Are you planning to attend my demo?"

"No," she said.

When he'd first met her, he'd decided she was blunt. Over time, he'd learnt to appreciate her honesty. "Perhaps you should."

She tilted her head. "You think you can teach me something?"

"A lot of things," he said.

"That's a bit arrogant, Damien."

He longed to hear the word Sir on her lips. "Is it? We can all benefit from continuing education."

"Setting the scene and an intro to flogging is for newbies."

"Really?"

"Have you heard complaints from my subs?" The words were tight, as if her breath were constricted.

"Not at all."

"Then?"

"I'm simply suggesting that some of the best dominants have embraced or at least tried submission."

"As you have?"

"Indeed."

Her mouth parted before she pursed her lips.

"I'd be happy to master you, Catrina."

"If you ever crave a beating, Damien, I'd happy to put the smack down on you," she returned.

"I invite you to try, Milady."

Brad entered through the kitchen door, and when Catrina saw him, she smiled. Damien wondered what it would be like to see that same expression directed at him.

The man shook snow off his gold boots before joining them. He knelt then placed his forehead on the floor in front of Catrina. "Good boy," she told him, crouching to rub his head.

Damien took Catrina's arm to help her up. Her skin was warm, inviting. If she felt the same jolt of electricity as he had, she hid it well. Against her ear, so no one else could hear, he said, "With your hair, you'd look stunning in that position."

She drew her dramatically sculptured eyebrows together as she scowled at him. Without a word, she extracted herself from his grip.

Just then, Master Lawrence arrived and joined them, nodding at Damien and kissing Catrina on the cheek.

"You're here, Master!" Bradley exclaimed.

At Lawrence's urging, Brad thanked Catrina as she relinquished the leash. The blond followed his master down the stairs at an enthusiastic trot.

"I'm available if you change your mind," Damien said to Catrina before moving off to meet his partner in the foyer.

Catrina might have muttered something about hell freezing over, and with the snow and cold, he figured anything was possible. He grinned. Victory would be a sweet reward.

* * * *

When Damien had disappeared from sight, Catrina exhaled. Damn him. Who the hell did he think he was? His words had shaken her, and she glanced around to be certain no one had overheard his outrageous proposition. As if she'd be on her knees for any man.

So what was it about him that sent flutter-kicks through her stomach?

Catrina had always prided herself on being in charge. From class president in high school to editor of the college paper, and now, as the founder of her own company where she focused on the financial success of women, she'd been outspoken and driven.

Early on, she'd also made the choice to be equal in her sexual partnerships. Her first experience taking the initiative hadn't been well received. Even now she cringed at the memory.

Not only had Todd objected when she'd tied his wrists to the headboard, but when she'd straddled his face, he'd demanded to be released. Towering over her and yelling, he'd said she didn't want to be treated as an equal, she was a control freak. When she'd tipped back her head and objected, he offered to tie her up and force her to lick his balls. She'd refused.

The next day, when she'd arrived home from work, his belongings had been gone from her apartment and his key had sat in the middle of the dining room table.

A few weeks later, she'd met a handsome blond man at a party, and he'd jokingly said he'd kiss her feet.

She'd taken him home, and he'd done just that.

Ever since, she'd been involved with good-looking men who took care of her every sexual need. She ensured they received everything they wanted and needed, too. What could be better?

At times, especially in the middle of the night, she pushed away the nagging voice that whispered she was missing intimacy. She'd toss and turn, telling herself she had friends for problem solving and conversation. Her life was full in every way. She didn't need anyone to hold her and connect with about everyday life events. And she didn't need someone like Master Damien Lowell bossing her around and making her kiss his feet. Definitely not.

Gregorio moved through the rooms, announcing the start of Master Damien's demonstration. Now that Master Lawrence had claimed Bradley, she was at loose ends. She could avail herself of the services of a house sub, and maybe even Gregorio with his pirate-like looks, silver earring and sexy body would agree to play with her. Since he was busy talking to a couple she'd never seen before, that would have to wait until later.

More out of boredom than curiosity, and not because Damien had issued a challenge, she snagged a sparkling water infused with cranberry juice and wandered into the living room.

The room's usual furniture had been removed. A couple of rows of fold-up chairs had been arranged in a semicircle near the fireplace. Many dominants sat, with their subs standing or kneeling near them.

She stood near the back. From here, she had a clear view of Damien and the pretty sub on her knees, facing him, her head bowed. Catrina appreciated the woman's lush, feminine form. She wore her hair in a blonde bob that shaded her face. The pair were turned sideways to the room, so that both of their expressions and all of Damien's gestures were obvious.

Gregorio entered and stood near Damien.

The gathered crowd quieted as Damien touched the woman's head.

Even from the distance, Catrina saw the submissive tremble. It took courage to participate in a demo, especially with the house owner. Her nervousness radiated in the room.

Catrina noticed his biceps flex as he made tiny massage motions. His silent communication was impressive.

"I'd like you to stand," he told the woman. "And tell us your name."

"Susan, Sir." She kept her eyes on the wooden floorboards, even as he offered a hand to help her up.

Warmth shimmied up Catrina's spine as she remembered the feel of his firm grip on her arm. She didn't normally accept help, and it had surprised her how much she'd liked it.

"I appreciate your show of respect," he said.

Damien had not used that tone with her. He'd spoken to her as an equal, not as a man intent on seducing a woman.

"And I'd like you to look at me," he continued.

The woman glanced up, her eyes wide and unblinking.

"I want you to be completely comfortable with everything we do here tonight."

"Yes, Sir."

In that same, reassuring, voice he went on, "Is there anything you're uncomfortable with?"

"I'd like to leave on my underwear, Sir," Susan whispered with her head turned.

He captured her chin and recaptured her gaze. "Of course you may leave on your underwear. Anything else I can do to reassure you?"

She shook her head but started to fold her arms.

"It appears there may be something else you're reluctant to tell me."

"Ah… I have very sensitive nipples, Sir."

"Then I'll treat your nipples with all due respect."

"Thank you, Sir." She gave a tentative smile.

"And do you have a safe word, Susan?"

"Stop."

"So, to be clear, stop means *stop*."

"Yes, Sir."

"And a slow word?"

"Slow, Sir."

"Got it. We'll take a break if you use the word slow."

"Thank you, Sir."

Sierra Cartwright

"You're also aware that Halt is the house safe word."

"Yes, Sir."

In that instant, Catrina understood why Damien taught demos at the open house events. It was one thing to inform Doms that they needed to make their sub feel comfortable, but Damien was genius. He was repeating what Susan said, but not in parrot-fashion. He soothed and built trust not only with the way he spoke but with physical touch. It was subtle and elegant. Maybe he had been correct in thinking she could learn something from him, as much as that thought rankled.

Transfixed, she took a drink while she watched him undress Susan. He could have ordered the sub to strip. Instead, he took the opportunity to squeeze her shoulders and run his fingers over the skin he bared. "Now I'd like to remove your bra."

Catrina gulped two quick drinks. The seduction in his tone made her wish the words were directed at her.

"Yes, Sir," Susan said.

He turned Susan so that her back was to him.

After he'd released the clasp, he turned her once again. Her shoulders were rolled forward so that the bra remained in place.

"Thank you for your trust," he continued, drawing the straps down her arms. "Remember you can stop or slow down at any time." When he'd removed the lacy black brassiere and handed it to Gregorio, Damien put his hands on her and said, "You're beautiful, Susan."

As if a switch had been turned on, she smiled, and her cheeks flushed with colour, making her look radiant. Hesitancy had been replaced with confidence, impressing Catrina.

She couldn't look away even if she'd wanted to, as he cupped Susan's breasts and flicked his thumbs across her nipples. Her eyes closed. As he continued, she moaned and moved towards him, curling her fingers around his wrists.

Catrina clutched her glass.

Shock tightened her throat. Damien's concentration seemed riveted on Susan. It appeared as if neither of them were aware of the dozens of people observing them.

For the first time, Catrina saw submission and dominance from an entirely different perspective. For them, nothing seemed to exist outside of one another, and Damien's attention didn't wander from the woman under his care.

Catrina took care of her men, meeting their needs. In return, she had at least one magnificent orgasm. Until now, that had been enough.

"Tell me what you want, Susan."

"An orgasm, Sir."

He smiled. "Oh, you'll most certainly earn that."

"Thank you, Sir." Her knees buckled.

"Can you wait?" he asked.

"If it's your desire, Sir."

"You're a very pleasing submissive. Tell me what we're demonstrating this evening."

"A flogging, sir."

"I'd like to make love to you with my flogger," Damien said.

As if she were the one standing in front of him, Catrina's insides melted. The man had hypnotic appeal.

"Yes, Sir."

Catrina had never looked at a man the way Susan was looking at Damien, eyes wide with trust and a reverence. What would it be like to…? With resolve, she shoved the thought away. She'd never know, and that was fine.

Damien led Susan to the hearth and placed her hands on the mantel. "Legs farther apart for me," he said, his words like a caress.

Susan moved into position.

"I can secure you in place, if you'd like?"

"I'll remain as I am, Sir, if that's okay with you?"

"Perfect," he replied.

She looked lovely, wearing only her panties. She'd been trembling earlier, but now, she was still. Though Catrina would never admit it, Damien's power even held Catrina spellbound.

Damien had said he wanted to make love with his flogger, and that's exactly what he seemed to do. He started with tender leather kisses, licking at the woman's shoulders and back. He let the strands fall in gentle waves.

Catrina had never wielded a handle with such skill. She told herself it was because a man's skin was much tougher than a woman's, but now she questioned if she'd assumed too much.

She watched as he brought Susan's body to life. He increased the intensity of his blows on her panty-covered buttocks. Her cries were whimpers of desire, not of distress. She appeared to surrender not only to Damien but to the flogger.

Goosebumps raised on Catrina's arms, and her skin tingled with anticipation. And she knew one thing. She didn't want to watch Damien please another woman.

Confused by the irrational thoughts careening through her, she gulped the last of her drink then slammed the empty glass on the tray of a passing server and headed towards the foyer.

"I'd like to be on the next shuttle to Winter Park," she told the submissive.

"It will be about twenty minutes, Milady. Jeff's just on his way back now."

Catrina nodded, said thanks then found the women's locker room. The place was empty, and she exhaled in relief. She took several minutes to smooth her hair, straighten her skirt, adjust her corset and splash cool water onto her face.

All that done, she felt more in control. She pulled back her shoulders and stepped into the hallway. Damien stood there, overwhelming the space, blocking her way.

She started to take an instinctive step back, but managed to stop herself.

Power cloaked him. For a moment she wondered what it would be like to play with him. Distressed by the idea, she shoved it aside.

"You were there," he said. "At the demonstration."

"I had nothing better to do."

"What did you think?"

She shrugged. "You know what you're doing."

"Weren't you curious to know what it would be like to be in her position?"

"Not at all. I can have a gorgeous man at my feet and tell him exactly what to do."

"Is that what you want? Or do you want a man who will concentrate all his efforts on pleasing you?"

"I have that now."

"Do you?" he countered. "Do your men give you the attention I gave Susan?"

"Of course."

"You ought to be spanked for that lie."

She shivered. With a stubborn tilt of her chin she snapped back, "How dare you?"

"You looked away before answering," he said. "When was the last time anyone cared enough to watch your movements so intently that they knew you weren't being honest? Aren't you curious about what you're missing?"

"No."

"Another lie?"

She shook her head.

He dropped his arms and advanced towards her. This time, she retreated. "Damien…"

"You know the house safe word," he told her. "You can use it at any time. But you aren't going to, are you?"

Jesus. *God.* What the hell was happening here?

Her back was to the wall. This close, she was overwhelmed by his masculine scent and determination.

His blue eyes were as dark as a twilight sky. A tiny pulse in his jaw mesmerised her.

"Is your pussy wet, Milady?"

"From what? Being near you? Watching your little demo? Not at all." She felt suffocated. And her pussy *was* wet. Damn it.

Impossibly, he took another step closer. With one hand, he captured her wrists and pinned them above her.

Her chest rose and fell as emotions tumbled through her. She shouldn't want to interact with him. With Susan, he'd been gentle, but there was nothing soothing in the way he held her, overwhelmed her. Then again, this was what she craved.

He touched the knuckles of his free hand to her throat.

She kept her eyes wide, pretending she wasn't affected.

His touch so gentle she hardly noticed it, Damien stroked downward, down the centre of her chest, bare skin to bare skin.

Then he traced beneath her right breast. He held her gaze, not blinking. She'd never had anyone's attention like this, and it was heady.

Even through her outfit, her nipple hardened when he moved over it.

There wasn't a part of her that wasn't aware of him.

"Open your mouth."

"Why?"

"Because I'm going to kiss you."

She started to protest, but he dived inside her. She expected him to coax her. Instead, he consumed her.

He forced his way in, tasting of persuasion and determination. The thrusts of his tongue made her mouth water. He insinuated a thigh between her legs, and despite her resolve, she rubbed herself against his leather-clad leg.

The woman in her recognised his mental as well as physical strength. This was a man powerful enough for her to trust. He'd never push her too far, but he would demand everything, that she hold nothing back, and maybe give more than she ever had to anyone.

As impossible as it was to believe, he deepened the kiss. She couldn't breathe. Couldn't think. And suddenly she didn't want to.

She felt an orgasm start to unfurl.

A Dom and sub moved past them, and Damien never allowed his attention to wander.

He kissed her until she began to shake.

As quickly as he'd started, he eased away. He adjusted their positions and hiked up her skirt. He moved a hand between her legs, and slipped beneath her thong to find her pussy.

"Your pussy *is* wet, Milady."

She shook her head, and he laughed. It was a satisfied, rather than triumphant sound.

"Shall I finish you off?" he asked, pressing a thumb to her swollen clit.

"I…"

"It's just you and me. I'll keep your secret. No one will have to know."

She wanted to refuse, should refuse. But she'd never known need this debilitating. Even if she found someone else or went somewhere to satisfy herself, it wouldn't be the same. She needed him.

He continued to make maddening circles on her clit, and he had one finger teasing her entrance.

"Do it," she instructed.

"Ask."

Damien was making it clear he was in charge, not her. No doubt he'd give her what she wanted, but her compliance would be the cost. "Yes," she said. "I'd like an orgasm."

When he didn't change the tempo, she closed her eyes. He allowed her the time and the space to wage her internal battle. Sensations assailed her, forcing her body to relax. She became a puddle of feminine need. "Please," she whispered.

"Look at me."

She did.

"Ask again."

She understood. He wouldn't let her escape or pretend she hadn't been aware of what she was doing. "Please, Damien. Give me an orgasm."

"My pleasure, Milady."

He circled her clit and inserted two fingers deep inside her pussy. He finger-fucked her as he teased her clit.

Her legs shook with the force of his movements.

There was nothing sweet about this, and it was beyond hot. "Damien." This man was watching her reactions and responding to them.

"Come for me, Catrina."

He pressed his fingers against her G-spot.

Mindless of her surroundings, she screamed as the climax crashed into her. He helped her ride it, keeping his grip tight on her wrists, pressing her against the wall, supporting her body.

"So, so perfect," he said.

She screamed a second time, shattered. Her body went limp, but she wasn't worried, he was there, holding her in a firm but tender grip. She trusted him completely.

It seemed like minutes later when she blinked and looked at him.

"Welcome back," he said.

"That was…" She held back the words, desperate to be on firm footing again.

"For me, too."

"I'm not sure I understand."

"I adore a woman who is so responsive. I appreciate you playing with me." He moved his hand from between her legs and straightened her thong and skirt.

She pulled her wrists free from his grip. "It changes nothing."

"Maybe not for you. It makes me want to know you more."

"Do you always use sweet words to make all the women swoon, Damien?"

"That was a scene, and you know it. This is different."

"Is it?"

He took her hand and placed it on his crotch. "You tell me."

"So? You have a hard-on."

"Were you born a cynic?"

She shook her head. "Life taught me."

"I can teach you other things, show you a different perspective. You'll be a better Domme for the experience."

"You did that to prove something to me?"

"Partially."

She wasn't sure if she was hurt or shocked or pissed. No man had ever taken control from her, and she was desperate to get it back. "At least you're honest." She put up a hand to push him away.

"The truth is, I did that because I wanted to get you off, because I'm attracted to you."

Just because he sounded sincere, didn't mean he was.

"Give me two weeks."

"What?"

"I'm challenging you. Spend two weeks with me, submit to me, see if the experience transforms you."

"Not just no, but hell no."

"What are you scared of?"

"Nothing scares me." Another lie. Plenty scared her, and with good reason.

"Then agree to it. You've got nothing to lose. You'll get new experiences, spend a few days up here, have a chance to relax in a way you never have."

"Relax?" She nearly scoffed.

"What would it be like if you could be yourself and let go, turn over control to someone else for a while?"

"I can't," she said, her heart thumping. That was as honest as she'd been with anyone, ever.

He inclined his head, showing he'd heard the fear in her voice. *Damn him.*

"Was it scary when I brought you off?"

She shook her head.

"When I made you ask for it?"

"No."

A woman entered the locker room without disturbing them.

"I will earn your trust, Catrina."

A traitorous part of her wanted to say yes. Instead, she met his gaze. His eyes were dark, probing.

He brushed a strand of hair back from her face. His skin held the faint trace of her scent.

She had to go before her resolve crumpled. "Thanks for the orgasm. My shuttle will be here soon."

He moved aside. As she walked past, he swatted her, catching the bare flesh above her stockings and below her buttocks.

Shock stole her breath. She stopped and rounded on him. Before she could speak, Damien had her against the wall, overwhelming her with his scent, his presence.

The sting receded, leaving a tantalising warmth that stunned her and made it impossible to string coherent thoughts together. Despite herself, she grabbed his shoulders and held on tight.

He leant forward and kissed her forehead before moving lower to graze her neck.

His gentleness surprised her, demolished the last of her defences. "Be at my place in Denver tomorrow night at eight," he whispered in her ear. "Just the two of us, Catrina."

"You know I can't."

"Eight o'clock," he repeated. "Be there."

About the Author

Sierra Cartwright was born in Manchester, England and raised in Colorado. Moving to the United States was nothing like her young imagination had concocted. She expected to see cowboys everywhere, and a covered wagon or two would have been really nice!

Now she writes novels as untamed as the Rockies, while spending a fair amount of time in Texas…where, it turns out, the Texas Rangers law officers don't ride horses to roundup the bad guys, or have six-shooters strapped to their sexy thighs as she expected. And she's yet to see a poster that says Wanted: Dead or Alive. (Can you tell she has a vivid imagination?)

Sierra wrote her first book at age nine, a fanfic episode of Star Trek when she was fifteen, and she completed her first romance novel at nineteen. She actually kissed William Shatner (Captain Kirk) on the cheek once, and she says that's her biggest claim to fame. Her adventure through the turmoil of trust has taught her that love is the greatest gift. Like her image of the Old West, her writing is untamed, and nothing is off-limits.

She invites you to take a walk on the wild side…but only if you dare.

Sierra Cartwright loves to hear from readers. You can find her contact information, website details and author profile page at http://www.totallybound.com.

Totally Bound Publishing

31609081R00144

Made in the USA
Charleston, SC
19 July 2014